I0723331

WRITTEN WITH PRIDE

STORIES BY QUEER AUTHORS

Edited by
**Fable Tethras, Viveca Shearin,
& Claudine Griggs**

Published in the United States by
Not a Pipe Publishing
www.NotAPipePublishing.com

Trade Paperback Edition

ISBN-13: 978-1-956892-21-5

TABLE OF CONTENTS

INTRODUCTION

Queer people are never truly safe. Whether it's fearing that someone will act on U.S. Supreme Court Justice Clarence Thomas's approval to revisit same-sex marriage rights, living in one of the 10 countries wherein being part of the LGBTQIA community is punishable by death, or enduring the vitriolic transgender abuse that is J.K. Rowling's twitter account, we are reminded time and again that our rights, safety, and peace of mind are always a matter of debate.

When the Parental Rights in Education Act (better known as the *Don't Say Gay Bill*) first entered public consciousness, many of us at Not A Pipe were aghast. Every 45 seconds, a LGBTQ youth (ages 13-24) attempts suicide according to The Trevor Project, and yet here was one more group trying to make it impossible for the most vulnerable members of our community to find support and compassion.

For many of us, we remember barely surviving those years ourselves. Many of us still struggle with depression and anxiety, or even endure abuses regularly. It almost feels as though every day the world gets a little darker, a little more dangerous for us.

So when one of our publishers floated the idea of an anthology devoted totally and completely to authors of our community, a group of us jumped at the chance to put some light back into the world.

Authors from around the world responded to our call for stories, and what came out of it was this book. Within these pages, you'll find tales full of magic, aliens, supernatural abilities, and even a few set in our world. Not all of them have happy endings, but all of them were penned by members of our community who still believe in their voice.

This book is to remind you that you're not alone. We may not know you, but we know you. We support you, and we hear you. We may not have the people to change laws, but we want to offer you what hope we can, and we can't wait until the day you can be completely safe simply being who you are.

-Fable, Viveca, & Claudine

FROM THE VINE

by Lina Gerhard

If Mom were here, she'd tell me she was right. That a camping trip was a *terrible* idea. That I couldn't run from the magic I had inherited, and especially not here.

I couldn't run from myself.

And she *was* right. But I certainly wasn't going to tell *her* that. It wasn't like the others listened to me, anyway. I'd wanted to go to the aquarium, but as soon as Kasey had said camping, that was that.

Now I was surrounded in the very place that made my blood prickle under my skin. A cathedral of flora— all of it watching me. My eyes darted from shaking tree branches to dark hollows, alert but finding nothing along the trail as I followed the others.

Then, something wrapped around my ankle, catching me mid-step and sending me to the dirt. My palms scraped across the rough pebbles and bits of twigs painfully, and I pushed myself up on my elbows, blowing an errant strand of hair out of my face.

Until now, I'd managed to avoid three vines along the hike... two miles that felt like a million. A quick, easy hike, according to Kasey.

"Why are we doing this again?" I huffed as I straightened my glasses.

Kasey spun from her place on the trail in front of me, hands gripping the straps of her backpack. Unlike me, she had a professional backpacking grade bag, one packed like a pro. Mine was so heavy that when nature attacked, I fell on my face.

"Because it will be fun!" she said, beaming down at me.

She reached a hand toward me, and I took it with a grumble. What she meant was the forest was her element. What she meant was this was a chance for her to be with Ben, who had foolishly agreed to come, while I hung out with Caleb, the one she'd only invited so I wouldn't be a third wheel. What she meant was she would be the leader, like always, and I would go along with it.

I almost felt bad for Caleb.

Kasey pulled me back to my feet and steadied me as my top-heavy bag nearly pulled me back down. Ben had stopped the wagon hauling our gear, like our food and tents, taking the opportunity to chug from his water bottle.

I readjusted my bag as Kasey turned back to the trail and Ben pulled the wagon forward. Movement along the ground caught my eye, and I looked down just in time to see another vine snaking along the earth toward me, determined to grab me again. I stomped on it, and it slithered away, disappearing back into the undergrowth as if it never existed.

This was going to be one exhausting trip.

Kasey and Ben turned to look at me, and I gave them a sheepish smile. "Bug on my leg," I said, blinking at them innocently.

Because how could I tell them the forest was out to get me?

Man, I hated nature.

I shoved a damp strand of hair out of my face and wrapped it around my ragged ponytail. My hair was too short to be contained, so it was stuck all over my face and neck. I was sure I looked just as attractive as Kasey had planned.

Caleb suddenly appeared from around a tree about twenty feet ahead on the trail, where it curved around a mass of boulders poking out of the dry brown pine needles. "You guys coming or what?" His gaze traveled from my disheveled hair to the dirt on my knees. "You okay there, Marge?"

"It's Margot," I said softly. But he'd already turned back to the trail. I rolled my eyes and hiked up my pack before following behind everyone else.

Yup, this was going to be fun.

I swatted a mosquito and shuffled along the path, avoiding the rocks and divots in the trail. Birds sang in the trees, but it sounded more like mocking, and I scratched at my arms as every chirp and buzz made my skin crawl. The air was hot and oppressive already, even though it was so early in the season that we'd still been sitting in classes last week. It clung to me like a film, and blood pulsed everywhere in my body to remind me how hot and uncomfortable I was.

By the time we reached the campsite, I could barely breathe and was covered in a layer of sweat. But everyone else seemed as cool and collected as when we'd left the parking lot. Was that really only two miles ago?

I lowered my bag to the ground and spent the next minute guzzling water while the boys and Kasey began unloading the wagon and tents. I dropped to a fallen log, legs shaking. Let them unpack. Let them set up. I was only here because I couldn't say no.

I shouldn't have come.

A leaf tickled my bare thigh, and I swatted it away, glaring at it as it recoiled back into the dead log I sat on. Hopefully it wasn't going to be a full weekend of this. When I'd called Mom from the dorms before the last week of classes to tell her about the trip, she'd told me to set wards, to protect the site, but... that was admitting she was right. Wasn't it?

Maybe I could convince Kasey to do it. Weather mages had the same ability to set up protective barriers as any other type of mage.

I leaned back and peered through the expanse of leaves in the canopy, each one seeming to wave for my attention. The sky was bright azure, but the clouds had taken on a cotton candy pink that said the sun was low. We didn't have much time to get the camp in order before we lost daylight.

With a sigh, I stood and brushed the dirt off my hands and butt, then made my way over to where Kasey was building our tent.

She glanced up as I approached. "Finally decide to help me?"

Her tone was light, and I smiled sheepishly. I grabbed a corner of the bright blue tarp and helped her shake it out and lay it flat on the ground.

"Sorry," I said with a shrug. "Told you I'd be no use."

She rolled her eyes. "Please. Like it's only about you being useful?"

I jerked my head toward the boys. "You think I don't know your scheme already?"

Kasey blinked up at me with wide blue eyes, the same color as the sky before a storm. "Whatever do you mean, Margot dearest?"

I shook my head and turned my attention back to assembling the tent pole, but even in my heat- and exercise-induced misery, I couldn't quite keep the smile from pulling at my lips. Despite her need to control everything (an all-too-common trait among weather mages like her), I had to admit she'd still always been there for me, from my first failed exam to me coming out to her as demisexual. Maybe graysexual. I was still figuring it out.

My smile faded. Actually, that kind of made the whole Caleb thing more annoying. I mean, she *knew* I wouldn't just click with a boy I didn't know, let alone want to distract him while she spent romantic time with Ben, but either she was too focused on her own pursuit to notice, or she didn't really understand what "demisexual" meant for me.

That, or it was just one more instance of someone not listening to me. That seemed to be a recurring theme.

I sighed as we finished setting up the tent, and she shot me a look, probing, wanting to know what I was thinking. I shook my head and turned to watch the boys' progress with their tent.

I almost laughed at the confused chaos behind us—tent poles askew, fabric upside-down, tarp half folded.

"We'd better help them," Kasey said mournfully, looking up at the sliver of sky through the canopy. "Or they'll be sleeping out in the open tonight. And there's a storm coming."

We somehow managed to finish setting up camp, collecting firewood—me while fighting off errant vines and branches—and lighting the campfire before the sun went down. Kasey handled that last part, summoning a tiny thundercloud to zap at the tinder.

The forest settled into night around us, darkness descending like a shroud until we couldn't see anything outside our ring of firelight and lantern light. Thunder grumbled in the distance, a long way off, but if Kasey's senses were right, we could be seeing it sometime overnight. The crickets chirped so loud that my ears rang, and I jumped every time an owl hooted or branch snapped.

I tried to settle on one of the fallen logs we'd placed around the fire, and Caleb passed me the marshmallows, already half gone. I offered him a smile I hoped was friendly but not inviting. I still had no idea what exactly Kasey had told him to get him to come.

Kasey set her lantern down and clicked it off, then took a seat across from me, next to Ben. I glared at her through the crackling flames, but she studiously ignored me. A tiny thundercloud hovered by her ear, its lightning flashes too bright in the absolute night of the deep woods. But it did remind me to ask her to set up protections around the camp overnight.

I popped a marshmallow into my mouth, eyes still on the darkness encroaching on our tiny circle of light, then stabbed a second one onto a pointy stick. I was too distracted by every rustling branch, every puff of wind, every distant rumble of thunder to even taste the sugar. A shame, really. I loved toasted marshmallows.

"How about a scary story?" Caleb said, leaning forward with a wicked grin. He waggled his eyebrows like dancing caterpillars in the flickering light.

My heart stammered at his words, stomach filling with butterflies. "Isn't it scary enough out here already?"

"Aww, don't be a spoil sport, Margie," Caleb said.

"It's Margot," I mumbled.

"Come on," Kasey said, glancing from me to Ben. "They are pretty traditional around campfires. And we did come out here for the full camping experience, right?" Her voice took on a note of urgency with her last thought.

"All right!" Caleb shoved the last bite of a s'more into his mouth. "Who'th firth?"

Kasey raised a finger, a devious look in her eye. "I have one."

The boys leaned closer, desperate to hear what she had to say. I pulled my marshmallows from the fire and tested them, swallowing down my fear as best I could.

"Do any of you know why this forest is called the Lost Mage Wood?"

The boys, entranced as they were, both shook their heads in unison. I shoved a marshmallow in my mouth, resisting the urge to roll my eyes. But a chill slithered down my spine anyway.

I knew this story, too.

"You really can't come up with a better one than this?" I said. I couldn't quite keep a tremor from my voice.

"Oh, calm down. It's just a story," Kasey said. Then she turned back to her enraptured audience. "Well, it was on a night much like this one. Hot. Dark. Stormy."

Something rustled by my side, and I nearly jumped out of my skin as a tendril of ivy reached for me. I pulled the leaf off the vine testily, and it recoiled, slinking away from me again.

"Minerva was just like any other student. Time filled with classes and extracurriculars. Boy crazy in the newfound freedom of college."

I rolled my eyes and choked back a sigh. Leave it to Kasey to assume every girl was boy crazy.

"One day, her ecology class took a field trip to this very forest, to collect plants from the deep woods. Only, Minerva was a plant mage. And she had no idea."

My heart stuttered. I wanted to press my hands over my ears, hide in my tent, run back home. Why did she have to pick *this* story?

"Normally, it's no big deal if a person doesn't know they're a mage. Unless you're a plant mage in the middle of the woods. You see, nature is unforgiving. Brutal. Plant mages have it in their veins... and nature wants it back.

"Minerva wandered just a little too far off the path and found herself separated from the rest of the class. But by the time she realized it, the forest had shifted around her, bending and changing to cut her off completely. It could smell the magic that flowed like her blood, and it wanted her.

"She tried to find her way back to the rest of the group, but every time she thought she heard them, the forest changed again, turning itself into a maze of vines and shrubs and trees. And her class couldn't find her either. She disappeared in these woods, almost to this very day fifty years ago."

I closed my eyes, squeezing them shut against the truth under the fiction of her story. Because my family used to have mages, too. And we all knew Minerva was real.

She'd been our last mage.

Though, Mom was convinced I was the next. But I couldn't be. We hadn't had one in our family for fifty years.

Not that Kasey would have any way of knowing any of that. The last time I'd tried to tell her about it, she interrupted me, and it never came up again.

"Legend says she's still here, wandering the forest, looking for anyone to save her from the woods."

A branch cracked deep in the trees behind me, and I jumped to my feet, half expecting to see a tree reaching for me next. My heart pounded so hard that my breath caught. Minerva was real, she'd really gone missing here, and Kasey may as well have just spoken her ghost into existence.

Why couldn't she listen to anything I said? Anything at all?

It seemed I wasn't the only one spooked by the story. The boys were also on their feet, staring into the woods in the direction of the cracked branch. But the darkness was too deep to see anything, whether it was a restless spirit or a squirrel.

Ben laughed nervously. "Good one, Kasey. How about another story?"

"No thanks." I bent down to pick up my sweatshirt and pulled it over my head. It was still over eighty degrees, but I was suddenly shivering. "I'm done with this."

"Margot, come on," Kasey whined. "You're being ridiculous."

I bit the inside of my cheek before I snapped at her. "Kase. We're in the woods, alone, and you're telling ghost stories. I don't like this, and if you guys insist on telling them, I'm going to bed."

She waved a hand at me with a scowl. "Fine. Go be boring somewhere else, then."

"Fine."

"Fine." She sat back down on her stump, pointedly shifting away from me. The tiny thundercloud floating by her head flashed at me threateningly.

I rolled my eyes and stalked toward our tent. I'd still be able to hear them through the fabric—fabric that wouldn't protect me from anything except maybe a little rain—but at least I could try to tune them out. I unzipped the tent and crawled in, sealing it behind me just as a tendril of ivy reached toward me. I shivered again, my heart thumping at yet another near miss.

No, I wouldn't tell Mom she was right. And I certainly wasn't like Minerva, no matter what Mom said.

I kicked my shoes off at the entrance to the tent, clicked on the lantern hanging from the center of the ceiling, and collapsed on top of my sleeping bag. It was a three-person tent, so with just me and Kasey, there was a small gap between the bags where our packs stood. I dug my ear buds out of the side pocket and shoved them in my ears. They wouldn't be enough to block out everything, but at least I wouldn't be able to hear their words without straining.

I closed my eyes and let the narrator of my current audiobook distract me from the cold fear prickling my skin. I shivered again and slid my legs under the sleeping bag as the voice droned on. It was a fluffy romance. Yeah, I know. An ace girl into romance? The thing was, these fluffy romances were a lot closer to my style than anything Kasey imagined for me. The ones I picked were either second-chance stories where the characters already had a foundational bond, or they developed a bond through the story. Really similar to how my own feelings developed: slowly, without attraction, and then a sudden realization, like a light flaring to life in a dark room, showing me what I couldn't see before. And while it wasn't a perfect representation of my feelings, it felt good to listen to someone else's story.

Plus, on a night like tonight, the fluff of a romantic comedy was a perfect counterbalance to Kasey's fearmongering.

The air shifted slowly as the storm approached, scenting the air with ozone and rain. I didn't hear the first drops hit the tent over the voice of the audiobook, but as the raindrops grew fatter and heavier, they shook the tent fabric around me.

And then a boom of thunder shook the ground, startling me out of the book.

I sat up, yanking the ear buds out of my ears and back into their charging case. I was about to run back out to the campfire to check on the others when Kasey tumbled through the door, zipping it up quickly behind her. Water dripped onto the canvas floor, and she pulled her shoes off before tumbling into the center of the tent. The tent swayed with the rain and wind, and she pulled the lantern down from the ceiling before it smacked her in the head.

She pushed wet hair out of her face. "Wow, it is really coming down out there."

Butterflies flittered around my stomach. "Are we going to be okay here?"

"Pft. Margot. I'm a weather mage."

She rolled her eyes and dropped to her sleeping bag, then closed them and lifted her chin toward the ceiling of the tent, inhaling loudly. Her hands moved through three of the weather mage hand positions corresponding to spells only they knew, cycling over and over again. As her hands and fingers danced in the bright, fluorescent light of the lantern, the wind and rain subsided. Even the thunder and lightning slowed, growing softer until it was merely a memory in the distance.

Maybe it would be cool to be a mage. There weren't that many of them, and they were crazy powerful. But then again, every mage I'd ever heard of could barely keep their own magic from killing them. I didn't want that kind of life. If I couldn't even get my best friend to listen to me, what hope did I have of getting magic to listen?

Kasey opened her eyes, shadows now under them to match those in the corners of the tent. "See? No problem." She stifled a yawn.

"Did you get rid of it?" I looked up at the ceiling as if I could see what she had done.

"Nah, that takes too much energy, and it can throw off the balance of the weather. I just hurried it along past us." She dug around in her pack for dry clothes.

"So... I know you told me not to ask, but... What do you think of Caleb?"

I suppressed a sigh. "He's kind of... I don't know. Why did you invite him? He can't even get my name right."

"You just gotta give him a chance." She nudged me with an elbow. "Maybe a kiss or two? Hmm?"

I shrugged, refusing to meet her eyes. "Kase. Do you hear yourself?"

I didn't wait for an answer. Instead, I shoved my ear buds back in my backpack and slid deeper into the sleeping bag. "I don't know about you, but I'm beat."

She blinked, her eyes already half lidded. "Yeah. Moving that storm took a lot out of me." She finished switching out her clothes and climbed into her own bag. "But we're still on for that hike in the morning. Don't think I forgot."

I sighed. "I didn't."

She reached over and clicked off the lantern. "Good. Because we're going. Night!"

The sun didn't come out in the morning. Instead, we were greeted with steely gray clouds and wind. I wasn't worried about rain or storms, not after Kasey's demonstration last night, but I already wasn't looking forward to this hike. The less-than-ideal weather didn't help.

Kasey was up and at the campfire making breakfast before I had even rolled out of my sleeping bag. I could smell the beginnings of whatever it was she was cooking even as I geared myself up for the hike. I pulled on knee-length denim shorts, an old, comfortable tee, and a green plaid flannel with the sleeves rolled to the elbows. I left it unbuttoned, unsure if I'd even keep it on for long. Right now, the air was humid and cool, but that could change quickly.

I laced up my hiking boots and stepped out into the morning air. It still smelled of rain, the earth dark with last night's storm, and a mist hung around the trees, reducing my line of sight to any potential forest attackers.

I made my way toward the fire where the boys helped Kasey cook up some powdered scrambled eggs. Delicious. But I still ate the portion that was handed to me. The trail ahead was probably tougher than I was prepared for, and I'd need the calories from a real breakfast.

Finally, we kicked dirt over the embers, poured some of the water from the creek to smother the last of the fire, and turned toward the trailhead off the side of the campsite. This trail would take us up the side of the mountain toward an overlook of the whole valley. Kasey said it would be worth the hike.

The three-hour hike. Uphill. Around boulders and drop-offs and wild animals. And then back to the campsite.

I took a deep breath as we stepped foot on the trail, steeling myself for the path ahead. Kasey immediately fell into step with Ben, leaving Caleb to walk with me. Another not-so-subtle attempt at distracting me, trying to make me feel less like the third wheel I was by setting me up with someone I was *not* interested in. Ignoring my wishes. And distracting me from the vigilance I needed out here among nature.

Caleb fell into step next to me as we trailed behind Ben and Kasey in silence. I tried my best to ignore the flirting in front of us, but it was hard when they couldn't seem to keep their hands off of each other.

"So, uh." Caleb cleared his throat. "Ben tells me you're a musician. What do you play?"

We were really doing this, weren't we?

"Piano," I managed to huff between breaths. We'd barely started, and I was already winded.

"Oh, cool. How long?"

I glanced at him. He looked perfectly composed, his breaths even and controlled. The only sign of his exertion was the flush in his cheeks. He seemed interested in my answer, but I didn't know him well enough to know if he was just being polite, just trying to ignore the PDA in front of us like I was.

I looked back at the trail underfoot and picked my way around a long, flat rock. "Sixteen years."

"Wow. That's really cool."

I didn't bother answering, still focused on the trail. With my luck, nature would attack as soon as I was distracted.

Caleb, to his benefit, took the hint and stopped trying to make small talk.

The trail was steep, and it took all my focus to breathe through the stifling heat of summer and watch out for invading vines or branches. Eventually, we stopped for a break, and I immediately bent in half, hands on my knees as I gasped for air. The others chatted and drank from their water bottles while I recovered, and I couldn't help but wonder again why they'd even bothered to bring me along.

And then something rustled in the undergrowth, rattling the briar-covered shrubs behind us. I straightened, holding my breath as I peered into the shrubs, hoping for something small and harmless, like a rabbit or squirrel. The small talk faded as my friends did the same.

Something green and leafy shot from the darkness of the bushes and wrapped around Ben's ankle. With a yank, he was on the ground and sliding into the trees.

"Ben!" Kasey shrieked, running after him.

I held up a hand and took a step toward her, just barely grabbing her arm before she broke through the briars after him. "Kase, no!"

Another vine shot out and wrapped around Caleb, pulling him away as quickly as Ben had disappeared.

As suddenly as it had begun, the forest fell silent, just me and Kasey standing together, still as deer in headlights.

Alone.

"What. The hell. Was that?" Kasey finally said, her eyes wide. I could practically feel her heart thundering along behind me, and miniscule storm clouds swirled around her head.

I swallowed, too afraid to answer, to tell her what was probably the truth. A truth I wasn't ready to admit... but it seemed I couldn't keep ignoring it.

As we stood there, the woods slowly returned to normal, the birds calling again, the normal hum and buzz of the insects filling the air. There was no sign of the guys, no hint that they had ever even been here at all. Minerva's story ran through my head in endless cycles. What would happen to them out there? Why had the forest taken them?

I took Kasey's hand and tugged her toward the woods. "We need to find them."

"Margot?" Kasey's voice trembled. "What's going on?"

I chewed my lip, hesitating. I didn't have an answer for her, at least not one I was comfortable voicing. "I don't know," I said. "But do you really want to just leave them out there?"

I dropped her hand to push back the branches of the shrubs, and she joined me, tearing branches away and stomping them to the ground to clear a path. Yet every time we cleared part of the way, it seemed to mend itself.

We moved faster and faster, pressing forward before it could close itself off again, and finally we broke through to a darker part of the forest where nothing but tiny white flowers grew out of the musty, damp earth. The smell of mold and dirt drifted around us, thick with the heat. Huge, old trees with smooth gray bark towered overhead, as still as statues... at least for now. I glanced over my shoulder at the shrubs we had pushed through, and they wove themselves back together before my eyes.

I took a deep breath and turned back to the dark woods, heart pounding. The forest knew I was here. And it wanted to keep me.

But I wouldn't be another Minerva. I couldn't. For one, I still had Kasey. For another, I wouldn't give in.

I *wasn't* a mage.

"What now?" Kasey said.

I glanced over at her. Her lip trembled, and my usually confident, powerful friend looked just as scared and young as I'd always felt around her.

Tearing my eyes away from her, I examined the ground instead. The plants hadn't left any trace of their passing... but the boys had torn huge gouges out of the dark, wet earth of the forest floor. A clear trail.

"This way," I said, setting out along one side of the trail, my steps more confident than I felt.

No matter how much I didn't want to admit it, didn't want to voice it, this was still my fault. Somehow.

"Are you sure about this?" Kasey said. "Maybe we should go back, get help. We don't know what caused this, so how do we know we won't be next?"

We won't. But again, I didn't say it.

Kasey turned back the way we had come, her phone already out of her pocket. But I knew as well as she did that there was no reception here; no one was coming for us unless someone hiked all the way back out to the car. So when I took another step in the direction the boys had disappeared, Kasey only hesitated a moment before following me.

The forest immediately around us was unnaturally still, too quiet, but not in a peaceful way. It was the kind of quiet that happens after a catastrophe, when everyone who witnessed it was still too shocked to move, to speak, to breathe.

I shuddered at the thought, and despite the heavy, hot humidity of the summer day, a chill wormed its way into my skin, burrowing for my bones.

Kasey waved her hands next to me, and I glanced over to see her strengthening her tiny pet thunderstorm into something bigger, more formidable. It rose to hover over her, darker than I'd ever seen it, the flashes of lightning within it pulsing quickly with the tiny rumbles of thunder that accompanied them.

Kasey caught me watching her. "Just in case," she said. "Whatever is going on... it's not natural."

It *was* natural, actually, but I merely nodded. It wouldn't hurt to have a little weather magic at our backs.

I turned my attention back to the path the boys had cut through the undergrowth, and we picked our way around the thorn bushes and vines that had been left flanking their trail. The thorns and briars grabbed at me, and I did my best to shake them off. Luckily, for now, the vines were content to watch like wary snakes from the branches overhead.

Green ferns slowly overtook the darkness of the old growth we'd passed through, and then a sea of ferns taller than my knees rustled in front of us. The path cut straight through the green.

I swallowed. If I stepped in there, there was no telling what would sneak up on me or what the ferns would do.

Not that they were out to get me or anything.

I looked left and right, but the ferns continued in an endless field as far as I could see, stretching forward until I couldn't pick out any individual plant anymore, until all I saw was a wash of green.

Kasey plunged ahead. "Come on."

"Kase, wait," I started. But she was already several steps in, once again not listening.

I took a deep breath and hunched down as I took my first steps, grounding myself in preparation for the unseen enemies that might lie ahead. The ferns brushed against my leg, and I shivered at their touch, cool and soft, beckoning me like a siren to allow them closer, to speak to them.

No. I wasn't what they thought. I wasn't part of them.

"So what's so bad about Caleb?" Kasey said, eyes on the ferns as she plowed through.

I glanced up at her, irritation clenching my jaw. With a conscious effort, I relaxed it enough to say, "What do you mean?"

"Well, you seem really annoyed at him all the time. But he's really nice. And you seemed to like him at the end of last year."

I almost rolled my eyes. I liked most people... until they gave me a reason not to. Caleb hadn't been an exception to that until Kasey tried to play matchmaker.

"He's fine," I said.

"So what's the problem? He really likes you. I'm sure he'd go out with you."

"Kase, I barely know him. We've been over this."

"What does that have to do with anything?"

I took a breath before I snapped at her. "How do I know I'm interested in him if I barely know him?"

"What does that matter?"

"I already explained this to you. You're not listening."

I could feel my anger rising. Was she being willfully ignorant, or did she really not understand? Sure, maybe eventually I'd like Caleb, but I had no way of knowing that this early. I wasn't attracted to him, and, as I told her, I wouldn't know if that was even possible until I spent enough time to really get to know him.

And I was sure he wasn't willing to wait for me to decide, judging from the way he seemed to jump from girlfriend to girlfriend.

Not to mention we really didn't have time to discuss this now.

The ferns shivered around us as if wind had swept through the woods, but the air was still. I swallowed down my anger, but it was too late.

The ferns were awake now. They might have suspected before, but now they knew I was here.

Now they could smell my blood.

I *was* like Minerva, and they would have me. I couldn't keep denying it. Not anymore. Not here.

I grabbed Kasey's wrist and started running, pulling her along after me. She resisted for a moment, but then the ferns reached for us, wrapping around our ankles, and even the trees shivered. Branches shifted with groans and creaks, and I dodged as one swept toward us.

Kasey didn't see it coming.

It hit her with a solid *thwack*, and we both tumbled to the ground as it took her out. The ferns clawed at me with their soft fronds, trying to hold us down, to keep us in their green sea, to drown us.

I tore the ferns off me then dug in the sea until I found Kasey. She moaned, holding a hand to her head.

A tree groaned behind me, and I glanced back just in time to see another branch swinging at me. I ducked, then grabbed Kasey's arm and pulled her to her feet.

"You okay?" I managed, unable to keep the fear from my voice.

"Yeah," she mumbled.

It was all we had time for. I pulled her back into the trail of destruction the boys had left through the sea, and we bolted the rest of the way to the other side, where the ferns thinned and the trees abruptly ended at the edge of a clearing. Every step of the way, we dodged branches, tore the ferns away from our feet. We even had to leap past a few vines reaching our way.

Finally we tumbled into the small clearing, blessedly free of anything other than short grass, probably gnawed down by deer or other forest creatures.

I bent in half, huffing and trying to catch my breath past the oppressive heat. Insects swarmed here, buzzing around our heads in irritating patterns, humming in my ear, fluttering their wings against my skin as they tried to get a taste of my blood, too.

Could they smell the green in it? The bits of Minerva that existed in me?

The buzz of the insects grew louder, cicadas chirping overhead, mosquitos flitting past my ears. Then another sound cut through the insects... a scream.

Kasey and I exchanged a look, then darted across the clearing in the direction of the scream. My heart pounded in my chest, and I panted for air with each step. Were they okay? Were they hurt? How much time did we have left? In a few moments that felt longer than an eternity, we plunged through bushes that grabbed at us, vines that tried to ensnare us, and more trees that ached to cage us.

And then the ground dropped out from beneath us. We tumbled down a steep incline, gaining speed as we rolled. I hit a rock with an elbow, then another rock jabbed into my ribs, and finally I hit the bottom flat on my back, driving the air from my lungs. I gasped, trying to catch my breath while my head buzzed like it was filled with bees. Slowly, I pushed myself up and felt around for my glasses. They'd fallen off somewhere on the way down, but I couldn't see anything clearly enough to spot them.

Cool plastic touched my fingers, pushed into my hand, and I instinctively grabbed my glasses and pushed them onto my face. "Thanks," I wheezed.

I glanced over at Kasey. She nodded grimly, rubbing a welt on her jaw, but she seemed otherwise unhurt. The ditch where we had fallen was mostly barren earth and stone, no sign of the boys or the plants that had grabbed them. Nothing but a pile of stones and a tangle of vines at the edge of more briar-filled shrubs.

Where were we now? After spinning down the hill, I wasn't quite sure which way we were headed anymore.

Something gleamed white under the vines, and I squinted, trying to get a better look as I straightened the glasses on my face. They were a bit bent from the fall, one of the lenses scuffed, but at least they were still usable.

Then the source of the gleam came into focus. A bleached white skull stared back at me with hollow eyes, the vines curled around it and moss sprouting from its planes until it was almost unrecognizable.

I gasped and shuffled back, but I didn't have long to dwell on why a human skull sat out here, covered in the forest.

Another scream pierced the air, and I leapt to my feet. I looked to Kasey, and she stared back at me, eyes wide and face pale. As one, we rushed toward the sound, plunging back into the undergrowth.

"When are you going to tell me what's going on?" Kasey huffed between steps.

I hacked at a shrub that had wrapped itself around my leg. "I don't know what you're talking about!"

We lunged through the last row of shrubs and stumbled to a stop.

"Then what's that?" Kasey shrieked.

She thrust a finger toward a web of vines creeping across the ground, straight for me. And at the other end, Ben and Caleb, suspended from a tree branch.

"Why are they after you, Margot?"

But there was no time to answer. The vines suddenly struck at me like snakes, and it was all I could do to dodge. Kasey pointed at the vines, directing bolts of lightning from her storm clouds. They zapped the vines, singeing them and releasing the scents of ozone and burning grass into the air. Across the expanse of writhing grass and vines, Caleb and Ben thrashed against their restraints, but it was no use.

We had to get them out of here. If we didn't, we'd end up just like Minerva.

Minerva... What if that skull was Minerva? Or what was left of her. A chill pierced into my core, freezing me to the bones.

I could almost see her now, fighting against the vines I fought now, struggling against the forest. In the end, she wasn't strong enough. In the end, the forest took her. Just like it might take me now.

Well, it might take me, but I couldn't let it have my friends. Even if one of them *was* only here so my best friend could spend time with her crush.

I slid to a stop, determined to end this before any of them got hurt. Even if that meant... even if it meant I had to accept the power I never wanted.

"Stop!" I yelled, squeezing my eyes closed.

The forest fell silent, not even Kasey's thunder breaking it, and I opened my eyes again to see all of nature frozen, angled toward me as if... as if listening.

Like the forest, three sets of human eyes swiveled toward me.

And then the forest broke loose, as if every leaf, every blade of grass, every tree wanted to tear me to pieces. I leapt to the nearest rock, out of reach of the waving grasses. Vines raced along the ground in my direction, and thunder rumbled as Kasey picked them off one by one.

I had to free Caleb and Ben, had to get them out of here.

I gazed across the clearing separating us, trying to chart a route that would put me in as little contact with the flora as possible.

"Cover me!" I threw over my shoulder at Kasey.

She nodded once, raising her hands to direct her bolts as needed, and I lunged for the first rock. My feet barely touched the ground as I went. My skin prickled, feeling the call of the plants all around me, begging me to give in, to let them have me.

But I was a plant mage. If I claimed the power... I could control them.

"No!" I yelled, bolting again.

I was almost there, only a few more steps. I leapt through the air, arms outstretched to grab the vines holding Ben, when something wrapped around my ankle, yanking me back and down to the ground. I hit the ground almost as hard as when we'd fallen down the incline, and stars flickered across my vision.

"Get up!" Ben shrieked. "Help! Please, Margot, do something!"

Do something? Do what exactly? Even if I was a... a plant mage, I had no training, no background in magic. I didn't know how to control the flora.

I would end up just like Minerva. I shuddered again as the image of those empty, hollow eyes wrapped in vines flashed into my mind again.

"Margot, get up!" Kasey yelled.

Anger flashed through me. Once again, even though *I* was the one with the plant magic, she was telling me what to do. Once again, it was her words over mine, drowning me out. The anger built like a flame, small at first, then engulfing me.

"That's enough!" I screamed, bolting to my feet. "For *once*, can I not do this without you bossing me around? For once can you please listen to me? Let me be the loudest voice?"

The grass trembled under my boots, shivering at my fury.

"You picked a camping trip when I told you how much I *didn't* want to go to the woods!" I went on, ignoring the shaking of the leaves in the bushes behind me. "I told you I didn't care if you and Ben dated, yet you did nothing but point out guys and girls you thought I'd be *cute* with. I told you I was asexual, yet you set me up with someone I didn't know, expecting me to, what? Hook up? Entertain him? Come *on*, Kasey. How many times do I have to tell you what I want before you listen to me?"

Something much larger rustled behind me, but I couldn't make myself turn to look. It was like a dam had burst, releasing everything I'd tried to let go, everything I'd tried to ignore for the entire semester.

"And now you're going to tell me how to fight a bunch of *sentient plants*?" I shrieked. "When is it enough?"

I spun toward the rustling in time to see the biggest Venus fly trap I'd ever seen rise up behind me, snapping its jaws, dripping juices from its mouth that, in a smaller plant, would digest flies or worms.

"I'm a freaking plant mage!" I shrieked, thrusting a hand toward the giant plant. "*I* say what goes here!"

The plant shriveled back, though I didn't understand why. Was there some power here I couldn't feel? Did it respond to my anger? My frustration? My determination?

Whatever it was, the entire forest listened now, shrinking away from me and my rage. Even Kasey did nothing more than stare, slack-jawed.

And then the Venus fly trap shrank back down to a normal, more manageable size. The vines suspending Caleb and Ben retracted, dropping them to the ground with a thud. The vines and grass gave a great shudder, then stilled.

The forest fell silent, and all I heard in the stillness was my own breathing, slowing gradually as my anger evaporated.

I'd done it. I'd said everything I'd held back for months. So now what?

A boot crunched on the leaves next to me, and I turned to Kasey. I bit my lip, waiting for her storms, her tempests, to wash over me, to carry me away with her own will. Like they always did.

"Margot?" she said, voice small.

I lifted my eyes to hers, hands clenched into fists at my sides. I swallowed, too afraid to say more than, "Yeah?"

"Have I really been pushing you around?"

I took a deep breath before answering. "Yeah, Kase. You have."

She nodded slowly, dropping her eyes. "And you're... you're a plant mage? Like Minerva?"

I shrugged. "Minerva was in my family, actually."

She nodded again, her face expressionless. "I'm... I'm sorry. I guess... I didn't get it. Didn't hear you. Didn't... listen." She lifted her eyes back up to me, and I almost cried at the pain I saw there. "Forgive me?"

I relaxed my fists and nodded, a tear leaking from an eye. "Always."

She jumped at me, wrapping her arms around me, and I hugged her back, closing my eyes and relaxing in relief.

I'd said it all, and things were... better? Better than they'd been before, for sure.

Something rustled by my foot, and I pulled back in time to stomp on a tangle of roots reaching up from the soil toward me. It shriveled back, and I sighed. Would it always be like this now? Would I always be at odds with the natural world?

Kasey glanced down where I had stomped. "I shouldn't have pressured you into this trip."

"Whatever," I said, turning toward Ben and Caleb, helping them to their feet. They seemed too stunned to do any more than stare. "But do you think we can maybe go home now? We can just do a backyard campout. At least... at least until I figure out how to deal with this magic."

I looked down at my hand, opening and closing my fist. It didn't look any different, but something felt different, and I needed to learn how to deal with it. How to keep asserting myself, advocating for myself, standing up for myself. If for no other reason than to keep nature at bay.

Kasey nodded and took Ben's hand. "Yeah. That's probably a good idea."

And for the first time all weekend, I smiled at her. A real, genuine smile. We were going to be okay, now that she was listening to me.

Now that I'd finally found my voice.

DOOM COOKIES AND DONUTS

by Marianne Xenos

Content Warning: Mentions of Assault

Central Square, Cambridge, MA, 1985, evening

Evi sat on a bench at the Joy of Movement Center watching the dancers hurry through the lobby. She kept her bag on her lap, not because she was afraid of theft, but because she wanted to hold it close, like a secret. She disliked crowds and felt both drawn and repelled by the savory sweat of the dancers.

A girl settled down beside her. Evi flinched and shifted to move, but paused and turned her head. The girl smelled unusual.

"Are you waiting for someone?" the girl asked, rummaging through the pockets of an oversized tuxedo jacket. She was pale and her spiky black hair revealed blond roots. Her black nail polish was chipped, and she looked like she'd stolen her older brother's clothes and her mother's drugstore reading glasses. Despite all that, she was weirdly beautiful. And she didn't smell savory. She didn't smell human.

Evi blinked and turned away.

"No, I'm alone," she said, immediately regretting her words. They sounded self-pitying, or worse, like an invitation. She tried to clarify. "I *like* being alone." She straightened her shoulders and looked out at the dancers. "And I'm not looking for friends, by the way. I absolutely don't need a girlfriend. Or a boyfriend." Evi paused uncomfortably. "Or *whatever*."

"*Okay*," the girl said, reapplying her black lipstick. "Awkward, maybe, but okay. I'm just sitting. Besides I've got plenty of friends—and more than enough *whatever*." Then she looked up and offered an enchanting smile. Enchanting in the original sense of the word. Magic sparked in her sky-blue eyes almost comically hidden behind the black plastic frames. Evi blinked again and didn't smile back.

She shifted in her seat. She wasn't used to small talk. She wasn't used to much talk at all, and she stared again at the dancers, and finally said, "You don't smell like them."

"You mean I don't smell like dinner?"

Evi took a second look at the girl. "How did you know?"

The girl shrugged. "I just know things. It's my *gift*." She rolled her eyes and drew quotation marks with her fingers. "My name's Hazel, by the way. My sister is taking an Afro-Caribbean class, and I'm supposed to wait for her here."

Evi glanced again at Hazel and felt sudden panic. She lived in a world where you were either the *dinner* or the *diner*, and this girl was neither.

The girl held her gaze for a moment. "Do you like donuts? I'm hungry, and there's a place across the street."

Evi paused, and then nodded.

They left a note for Hazel's sister and went across the street to Harvard Donut. The sun had set two hours ago, and Mass. Ave. was dark, but still busy with pedestrians and traffic.

Evi and Hazel looked like two goth teenagers hanging out in Central Square. For Evi, the goth look came naturally. She was ivory-skinned, dark-haired, and dressed for stalking in the shadows. Hazel had to work harder.

"I'm usually offended by goth chicks," Evi said, tearing her chocolate-glazed donut with sharp, black-polished nails. Evi ate sugar and carbs about once a week. Other than that, she was on a purely liquid diet. "Maybe I'm being offensive, but goth chicks are mostly 'normals' in whiteface—doomcookies and tourists. I want to snarl at them—*just be yourself!*"

Hazel put down her grilled blueberry muffin and wiped her mouth before she spoke.

"You're going to have to do worse than that to offend me. I once had an evil freak suck the colors out of my brain."

"No...really?"

"Uh-huh, so, go ahead, call me a doomcookie or a goth wannabe. But when I'm myself, people gawk—strangers try to touch me. It's like they want to take me home as their pet Tinker Bell."

"Humans hunger for magic," Evi said.

"But not you," Hazel said leaning over her empty plate. "And I like that."

Evi considered her. "Well, it helps that I can't eat you." But she knew the truth was more complicated. She searched for something normal to say, something human and mundane, but she failed, and just stared at Hazel's eyes instead. The blue reminded Evi of October, of a late-afternoon sky promising all the colors of sunset. The memory of the daytime sky surprised her, and she almost smiled, but then she thought of the freak who had stolen Hazel's colors and she frowned instead. She put her napkin to her mouth, holding back her words. Was it wrong to talk about monsters over donuts? She put down the napkin and pulled her bag on her lap.

Hazel asked, "What's in that bag that's so special?"

"It's a secret." Evi said, with a hint of a smile. "Let's go back and I'll show you."

They paid, and Hazel left a hefty tip. Then they crossed Mass. Ave. and walked back to the Joy of Movement.

Hazel's sister was still in class, so Evi led Hazel to a studio in the back. Through the door they heard a show tune from the 1940s and the rattle of metal-tipped shoes on the hardwood floor.

"Wait! Wait, and let me use my *gift*," Hazel said. She put one hand on Evi's bag and the other to her forehead, posing dramatically. "My psychic senses tell me these are tap shoes! You have tap shoes!" Hazel laughed, and finally Evi did too, letting her fangs flash in the dim hallway. Hazel tried a few dance steps, looking like a raggedy Fred Astaire in her tuxedo jacket.

Back in the lobby, they collapsed on the bench smiling, and Evi hugged her bag to her chest. She wasn't used to laughter, and it felt like a forgotten language. Like the memory of the sky in October. She had been a teenager in the North End of Boston when she'd been turned more than five decades ago. She'd had cousins and friends. At night, they turned off the lights in the living room and listened to radio shows in the dark. Evi loved comedies then, but dance routines were her favorite, especially tap dancers like Ginger Rogers or Ann Miller. The sharp percussion of tap filled the room, and her imagination filled the unseen parts of the performance—costumes, make-up, and setting. After she became a hunter, she pushed those memories aside. The dark took on a more serious meaning.

Evi felt her awkwardness return.

Hazel was still smiling. "Evi?"

Evi crossed her arms and looked at the floor.

"Evi? I'll do it if you'll do it."

"Do what?"

"Tap shoes, dancing! Maybe...maybe we can take private lessons, so you won't be bothered by the other students. This place must smell like a smorgasbord in spandex." Hazel nudged Evi's arm and widened her bright, enchanting smile. "Or maybe a pupu platter on pointe?"

Evi looked away and said, "Sorry, I'm suddenly feeling uncomfortable."

"When *don't* you feel uncomfortable?"

Evi looked up. "You don't understand, Hazel. You and I are different. My culture is strict. Not my birth culture, I mean....my birth culture was loud—Italian—all chatter and cousins and banging pots. But since I was *turned*...." She paused, and lowered her voice, "My kind are hunters. We know to be silent—not to smile, not to show our teeth. We eat in private with only our prey for company. And we move gracefully—furtively like ballerina ninjas—always in the shadows. Rubber soles on our shoes. Drawing attention to ourselves is...dangerous. It's death."

Evi turned away, horrified that she would cry, but she suddenly blurted, "Why did that freak suck colors from your brain?" Evi wanted to deflect and talk about somebody else's pain. It was unkind, but it worked, because Hazel tensed before she replied.

"Probably for the reason any psychopath does anything. It's like you said, 'humans hunger for magic.' And he thought his hunger was more important than my life."

The silence settled between them, and Hazel continued. "There are people who steal magic from my kind, and teenagers are especially...vulnerable. I didn't even know what I was! Not until I was attacked. One day I thought I was just an overly sensitive kid—artsy, queer, and a bit of a weirdo—and the next day I found out that I was literally magical. Just an old-fashioned fairy."

Evi glanced up to see Hazel's self-deprecating smile, then looked back at her hands. Unlike Hazel's chipped manicure, Evi's nails were filed long and sharp, coated with glossy black polish. She flexed her fingers once, thinking of Hazel's attacker, and then folded her hands again to listen.

Hazel took a breath and continued. "I only found out I was half-fae because the freak *harvested* my magic. We generate magic through vision, color, and imagination, and some genius figured out how to steal it, suck it out of our brains to become younger, stronger, or more virile or something. Or they sell it to the highest bidder."

Hazel sat back and closed her eyes for a moment. Then she opened them and rolled her shoulders, taking a breath. "Long story short: he got away, and I survived."

Evi pulled her bag close again, and they were both silent. The lobby was empty. Sound spilled from the various dance studios. Evi struggled with a tangle of feelings—compassion, rage, shame, and protection.

"Just so you know, I don't prey on humans anymore. I, um...I hunt other monsters." Evi said with an uneasy mix of defensiveness and insecurity. "That's why I moved back to Boston. Nobody knows me here now. But I only hunt the hunters."

Evi didn't look at Hazel, because she didn't want to see pity or disgust in those startling blue eyes. And she didn't want to see admiration, because there was nothing admirable about deciding how to live on a food chain. She just wanted to communicate, but it had been a long time and she was out of practice.

"And this monster who hurt you—I would hunt him down. I would slay him—destroy him—and spit his blood into the night."

Hazel leaned and touched Evi's hand with one finger, tentatively, as though charming a wild animal. "I know you would," she said quietly, "And I think that's totally freaking adorable. You are so fierce! With your talons and your teeth!"

Evi smiled despite herself, "No, Hazel. *You're* the one who's fierce."

Hazel said in a low growl, "And spit his blood into the freaking night!"

Then they were both laughing again, and Evi covered her fangs with her hand. Two very human girls in leotards and leg warmers turned to stare, which made Hazel laugh even harder. Finally, they fell into a comfortable silence. One class let out and another one started.

Hazel finally said, "Can I see your shoes?"

Evi nodded. She unzipped the bag and revealed a pair of shiny patent leather tap shoes with big black bows.

Hazel took them. "My sister works at a bar on Brookline Ave. It's called ManRay, and she has a key. And my aunt, who happens to be a part-fae witch, is a dancer—and the least judgmental person I know."

"What are you saying?" Evi struggled if somebody wasn't direct.

"I'm saying this: dancing in the dark with tap shoes and a disco ball."

Evi's eyes widened. "Just us?"

"Just us, and the teacher, and my human sister who you will promise not to eat."

Evi looked at the shoes. "When?"

The following Tuesday, in the early hours of the morning, Brookline Ave. was dark and deserted. Hazel, her sister Shea, and a woman with a boom-box who introduced herself as Aunt Jenny met Evi outside of ManRay. The air in the club was still and empty, alcohol and stale smoke cutting the salty smell of human sweat. The sister left them alone in the main room while she went back to the office to do paperwork.

Hazel had attached metal taps to the soles of her thrift-store cowboy boots, and Evi brought the shiny patent leathers with black bows. In the dim light, with just the disco ball winking from the ceiling, Jenny led them through some basics: tap, shuffle, toe-heel, step-ball-change. Then Jenny put on a tape, and the three of them—the vampire, the fairy, and the witch—clattered in the dark.

Evi closed her eyes, listening to the percussion of the other dancers' feet, creating rhythm and counter rhythm. Aunt Jenny understood the intricate shuffles and riffs of tap dance and she provided a rhythmic structure for the others, allowing them to improvise. She cued tapes on the boom-box, everything from Doris Day to Madonna, and slowing down with the Smiths. Evi felt clumsy at first, unprotected and exposed by the noise.

ManRay had go-go booths, raised open cages on black pedestals, and she climbed up and stood in the soft shadows for a moment, letting her senses open over the base of rhythm. Hazel's rhythms were distinctive and her smell was already imprinted on Evi's mind. In the sparkling light of the disco ball, a shimmer of color surrounded Hazel like a cape. Evi imagined her own cape, something extravagant to match her black shoes and nails, with rhinestones glinting like prisms against the black.

Evi closed her eyes and remembered the old RCA radio in the North End, listening to Ginger and Ann while her relatives clattered pots in the kitchen. Then she relaxed in the dark, focused only on sound, and she danced.

THE WAY I SEE IT

by Tucker Struyk

Content Warning: Racism, Threats of Violence, Violence

Banners and picket signs lined the block in front of Red Cloud Middle School. People rattled off formulaic chants at Mrs. Quirke's car passing by. Their faces were obscured by trucker hats and face masks—only their wide eyes and creased foreheads were seen. Mrs. Quirke cast her own baleful gaze over the crowd. A couple protestors pointed at her Prius, as they snickered and jeered. She parked in the teacher's lot.

The moment she opened her car door, voices permeated the air. A cacophony of insults and catchy phrases billowed from the crowd. "Keep critical race theory out of our schools," shouted one person. "My child, my choice," cried another. The chicken scratch scrawled on their placards repeated those sentiments. Some in cruder words than others.

Mrs. Quirke tucked her chin to her chest on her walk inside. Her eyes fell to the ground in front of her feet and stayed low, but demonstrators remained in the periphery. She recognized that angry prattle enjoyed an audience. Better to ignore the ignorant. There was no reasoning with the ignoble.

Mrs. Quirke wrote out the date September 28, 1919 on the chalkboard. Her chain link bracelet jingled with each chalk stroke. "Does anyone know what happened on this day?" The students sat with their heads in their hands. "I'll give you a hint. It happened right here, in this city." She turned on the classroom projector. "No one?" The image displayed a horde of people who surrounded the front doors of a building with individuals dangled from the façade and shattered glass in the windowpanes. "This was the start of the Omaha race riot."

Mrs. Quirke clicked on the next slide and projected an image of a man, in the middle of the street, engulfed in flames. His body splayed atop a bundle of burning scrap wood. The students sat upright in their seats. "This was the day Will Brown, a black man, was denied his right to a fair trial," said Mrs. Quirke.

"Instead, a white mob surrounded the Douglas County Courthouse and forced those inside to hand Mr.

Brown over for their own safety. The police officers, city officials, and even the mayor were made prisoners by thousands of angry citizens." Mrs. Quirke's arms fell to her side with a defeated thud. "Eventually they caved in on the demands. Mr. Brown was thrust from the courthouse and handed over to the gang." Students lurched forward in their combo desks. "He was lynched. They hanged Will Brown from a lamppost at the corner of 18th and Harney."

Mrs. Quirke caught a glimpse of a student's phone screen. A blue light glowed under Briar's desktop. "Mr. Dempsey, is there some kind of emergency?" she asked.

Briar slid the phone under his leg. "No, Mrs. Quirke."

"Then, why are you texting in my class?" She pointed at the screen. "Is this not enough to hold your attention?" Briar blushed. "Hand it over," she told him. Briar obliged her, but rolled his eyes. "You'll get it back at the end of the period."

As she walked back to her desk, Briar's phone vibrated in her hand. In the message, she saw a link with the headline of a Media Wars article. It read "Liberal Lies: The Holocaust Hoax." The text came from the contact of a fellow student, who Mrs. Quirke taught the semester prior. She lifted her head and saw protestors in the window. They marched off down the street—signs held high, like raised fists. She turned away and tossed Briar's phone onto a pile of ungraded papers. The warmth of the phone's battery was still present on her skin. The class turned to one another with befuddled looks.

"As I was saying," said Mrs. Quirke, "discussions of race in a classroom setting is not a novel idea and remaining ignorant to history will not protect you when an angry mob decides to knock at your door." Her steely eyes met Briar's. "We must reflect in order to progress."

Mrs. Quirke picked through the arugula for bites of fresh fruit and chicken. She looked up from her salad to find Principal Grundy in the doorway. She gulped. "Knock, knock," said Principal Grundy. "Is this a good time?"

Mrs. Quirke wiped salad dressing from her lips with a napkin. "Of course," she said. "Please, have a seat." She gestured to the closest desk. "What can I do you for?"

Principal Grundy remained on her feet. Her steepled hands held above her bootcut trousers. "Listen," she said, "I've been getting some complaints from parents about your recent lessons."

"If this is about the Omaha race riots," said Mrs. Quirke, "I'll have them know that the Will Brown lecture has been in the curriculum since I was a teacher's assistant for Mr. Willard."

"I hear you." Principal Grundy smiled. "I'm on your side." She raised her shoulders to an ambivalent shrug. "I just think we should consider alternative lessons at the moment." Her hands separated into dismal swats through the air. "You know, with all these protests going on."

"Prudence, the course I teach is meant to cover state history. Wouldn't I be doing the children a disservice by ignoring the uncomfortable parts?"

Principal Grundy cleared her throat. "Ultimately, you would be doing Red Cloud a disservice." She shook her head. "I understand you wrote a book on the subject of Will Brown, and that must be frustrating to go through what you did, but we can't handle anymore backlash from the parents. Not in this climate."

"So I should toe the line for the parents' sake?" Mrs. Quirke ceased to blink. "They already banned my book from the library." Her eyes strained for moisture but were firm in their resolve. "If teachers aren't allowed to challenge students, who will?"

"I'm suggesting you keep an open mind to what they want from their child's education. Just until things calm down."

Mrs. Quirke's feet carried her forward momentum. The rubber soles of her shoes landed with smooth footfalls. A rapid cadence of flat-footed steps. The impact thrummed through her calf muscles. She heard a familiar bird song between lulls in the podcast on her phone. A tune she had not heard in months. After a long winter the robins had returned to reap the benefits of spring.

A woman on the trail waved at her. She pulled out a headphone from her ear. The woman crossed over to Mrs. Quirke's side of the trail with flyers in her hand. An old man stood at the woman's side. "Good morning," said Mrs. Quirke.

The woman extended a flyer to Mrs. Quirke—some pixelated image of conspiracy theorist, Peyton Carnell, printed on colored silk paper. "Hello there," she greeted. "Do you want to hear about a website for humanity?"

"I'm sorry." Mrs. Quirke doubted her own hearing. She removed the other headphone from her ears. "What was that now?" she asked.

The old man wrapped an arm around the woman's shoulder and reeled her back to their side of the trail. His eyes lowered. The woman went on, "There is a spiritual war in this country that the lamestream media won't even talk about." She shook the paper in her hand and used a thumb to draw attention to the Media Wars website listing. "Educate yourself."

"Oh," said Mrs. Quirke. "I'm not interested. Thank you."

The woman placed the yellow sheet back on top of the pile. She pulled her eyeline away from their conversation with her nose turned up. The old man moved his arm to the small of her back and shoved her forward. He gave Mrs. Quirke an apologetic look. "Have a good day," he said. They continued their walk.

Mrs. Quirke shook off the encounter and jogged to the edge of Clift Park, where the unfinished trail dead-ended at a creek. Plans for bridge construction in this area were abandoned years ago. The trail was not maintained beyond eye sight of the soccer field. Weeds and turfgrass overgrew the concrete edges. The path was narrowed to the point that no bikers or joggers came through the area.

At the end of the trail, she stopped to take in the view that overlooked a small confluence of streams. Her eyes drifted from a paddling of ducks in the water, to a conspiracy of ravens in flight—until bright lettering caught her eye. On a nearby utility pole, the words read "Media Wars" in a bold font. Mrs. Quirke scoffed. She glanced over her shoulder. The woman and her consort were nowhere to be seen. She picked at the sticker's corner and peeled it off from there. Underneath, the rectangular outline remained. She hoped it was not there for long.

Mrs. Quirke overheard bitter conversations by the instant pot. Protests ensued and people complained, yet she kept to herself. The teacher's lounge coffee sputtered out in clumpy dribs. By the time she entered the classroom with a hot thermos and a stack of papers in her arms, she was late. She scanned the scene. The students chattered as though she was not there. A group of boys congregated around Briar's desk in the corner of the room. His garrulous speech and smug smile charmed the crowd.

"…what about satellites then?" asked a student.

Briar chortled. "It's a load of crap." He raised a brow. "The liberal elite won't let us know how their deep-fake technology works or how long they've had it." His chair tilted backward on two legs. "Don't be sheep." He pulled up a picture on his phone to show off. "Look," he said. They leaned in. A dumbstruck look befell their faces. "I'm telling you, don't believe everything you're told. The world is flat."

Mrs. Quirke projected a malefic glare across the room. Each student who felt her presence was consumed by silence. She saw the class with sober eyes—mere children scrambled to draw associations between the fragmented notions they could grasp. She tossed her purse onto her desktop. "Mr. Dempsey," she said. Her arms crossed. "It appears you have a presentation prepared. Perhaps to make up for the model UN project you 'forgot about.'" Students chuckled. "Why don't you share it with everyone?"

Briar grinned. His shoulders raised in a playful shrug. "I don't know," he said. "It doesn't exactly fit your woke agenda."

"Yes, I'm aware of your struggles with the concept. As I understand, you've struggled to stay awake all semester."

The class burst into laughter.

"All right. Fine." Briar stood from his chair and marched behind Mrs. Quirke's desk. "Why don't you let me teach the class for today?" He fumbled with the laptop cable insert and extended his arm for the projector remote just out of reach. "I'm sure I could find something worth our time."

Mrs. Quirke threw her head back, sniggering. "I'll check out your sources when you manage to pass this class." Red formed at Briar's earlobes and ignited his face in crimson. "For Christ's sake, you can't even name the vice president and I'm expected to conform to your narrow perspective on the world." She thumbed her nose. An ache prickled at her temples. "For now, it's safe to assume the bulk of your lecture could be found on Media Wars or, God forbid, coming out of your parents' mouths." Mrs. Quirke dug her heels in. "What is wrong with this generation? Do you know reality from myth?" Briar took his hands off the keyboard. His eyes darted in furtive glances—from Mrs. Quirke to the floor.

Quietude enshrouded the room. Mrs. Quirke looked away from Briar's rose-colored cheeks and found the class frozen in place. Two students recorded her from their phones. Realization crashed into her. She withstood the tide, as a buoy in high waters, but rally cries rang in her head from protestors she passed on her way in. "Say no to CRT," they said. "Say no to hate." Over and over again. Eventually the tide severed her anchoring link and took her out to sea. She shooed Briar off to his seat, then withdrew to her desk. She ordered the students to turn their phones off, then hid behind her screen. Even as her lecture began, the voices never left her. The headache magnified under ultraviolet bulbs, like a lesion exposed to stagnant water.

Mrs. Quirke took a seat. Family photos and sticky notes adorned the L-shaped desk in front of her. Principal Grundy drummed her fingernails against the mousepad. "You know why I called you here," she said. "I warned you about this, Cassidy." Her fingers became still. "You just couldn't leave well enough alone."

"I know. I'm mortified." Mrs. Quirke tucked her hair behind her ears. "I'm sorry," she said. "I don't know what came over me."

"You humiliated a child," said Principal Grundy. "I saw the video. Hell, half the school board has by now." She paused. Her eyes did not blink. "This is a mess, you understand?" Mrs. Quirke nodded. "Exactly the kind of situation I was trying to avoid when we last talked." Those glinting eyes zeroed in on her. "How does this make Red Cloud look?"

Mrs. Quirke frowned. She worked there long enough to know Principal Grundy wanted to see her grovel. She humored her. "I blemished Red Cloud's upstanding reputation," she said. Her hands folded on her lap. "In the moment, I lost hold of myself. I don't even remember everything I said or why I said any of it." Tears lodged in her throat. She swallowed them. "I hope you can find it within your heart to let me make up for my mistakes."

"You've worked here ten years with no issue." Principal Grundy's eyes softened. "What's gotten into you?"

"Thirteen years, actually." Mrs. Quirke tried to smile but her lips failed to move. "I feel like everyone's out to get me." Her grip tightened around her thumb until blood flow stopped. "Like there's some grand Media Wars cabal at play." Principal Grundy shifted in her chair. "I know I'm not making much sense," said Mrs. Quirke. "I can't think straight anymore." Her laughter came out warbled. "I haven't had decent sleep in a while."

Principal Grundy reached over the desk and put her hand over Mrs. Quirke's. "I think you should take the rest of the week off." She grinned. "Just relax. Take your mind off things. Okay?" Her smile faded. "Maybe look into a sleep aid, if you're really having trouble."

Protesters gathered in their usual spot. Mrs. Quirke locked sights on her parked Prius and did not veer from it, but she felt eyes cast on her as she walked. Murmurs spread over them like birds atwitter. They turned from the street to the teacher's parking lot—swarmed in a faceless mass. They weaved by light poles and parked cars to block her in. Mrs. Quirke caught wind of their plan. She quickened her pace.

"People like you are what's wrong with this country," said one objector. "God forbid parents like us have a say on who teaches our children," another mocked from the crowd. A woman ran with a toddler cradled in one arm and a picket sign in the other. Anger shriveled her face to a spoiled peel. Her cracked lips puckered at the seams. "Keep Dems out of our schools."

Mrs. Quirke fumbled to take car keys out of her pocket and press the button. Their footsteps bounded nearer. She lunged into the driver's seat, locked the door, and floored it in reverse. Once she made off onto the road, they stopped. She exhaled. Her hands shook. The steering wheel rattled in her grip the whole way home.

A jagged branch snapped in the jaws of the pruner. Afterward, Mrs. Quirke wiped the blades with an alcohol soaked rag. She thought better than to spread a disease through the garden. She does not know what blight the old wood may carry. Her body creaked and mouth groaned, as she clambered down ladder rungs.

Under the flowering dogwood, sat a nymph statue beside a reading bench—a gift from her late wife. Some peace offering made in the throes of a squabble neither would remember in a week's time—now, a weathered remnant of love long lost. The nymph's tilted head obscured her impassioned leer. Mrs. Quirke was drawn in. The figurine's contrapposto pose aroused a prudish smile upon Mrs. Quirke's altogether gloomy countenance. She took a load off with the dyad before she moved on to the next tree. Sleep lined the rims of her eyes, her eyelids heavy.

An alert sounded off in her pocket—mail from an unknown sender. She opened the email. The subject read "Watch your back" in capital letters. Images flooded the screen as she scrolled. A photo taken of her front door. Then one zoomed in on her address. Another at her backyard gate. The words "There is no safe space" typed beneath. She surveyed the property, but saw no one. She tiptoed toward the back door, the pruner wielded in hand as she stepped inside.

Pistols lined the showcase under laminated glass. A Gadsden flag strewed the wall. Mrs. Quirke hovered over a Smith and Wesson revolver as the man behind the counter stood akimbo. His absent-minded eyes lingered on her *Hamilton* face mask. "Excuse me," said Mrs. Quirke. "Which would you recommend to a beginner?"

"For girls," he said, "a nine millimeter."

He let her hold one to get a sense of the gun. She lined up the sights. Her arm raised to take aim. The weight felt good in her hand. "How much for this one?" she asked.

Five knocks pounded in "Shave and a Haircut" rhythm. Mrs. Quirke lifted her head from a Malcolm Gladwell novel and a warm fireplace. She squinted at the clock. Her blackout drapes drawn for the afternoon. She got to her feet and stopped at the welcome mat. "Who's there?" she asked. Her eye pressed against the peephole, but the shapes were hard to make out. She unlocked the door and poked her head outside. Her eyes widened beneath their taut brow. There was no silhouette on the doorstep. No stranger in the bushes. Only the face of Peyton Carnell, plastered on the columns by two torn bits of Media Wars tape.

Night closed in on the sleepy suburb, but Mrs. Quirke stood wide awake at her living room window. An email buzzed. Another disgruntled parent. This one claimed to find errors in their child's grade. She shut off her phone. Streetlights dappled the road in lucent specks. Neighbors spoke on front porches, as children cavorted on lawns and occasionally spilled out to the street. On TV, the nightly news played footage from Mrs. Quirke's class and read from social media posts. People condemned her. People praised her. Some names she recognized, most she did not.

She popped the cap off a prescribed bottle of Ambien. The coral colored pill sat in the palm of her hand, sank into the ridges and folds of her skin. Its weight was heavier in her grasp than in the bottle, but she remembered what Principal Grundy said—and her toffee-nosed smile when she said it. Mrs. Quirke gulped the tablet down with a sip of chamomile tea, shut off the TV, and went to bed with her book in hand. The words eased her to a serene state. Once the pill took effect, she opened the drawer on her bedside table.

Inside, the pistol rested on a bed of unread papers. She checked the cylinders. Each was loaded. Just as she closed the drawer, shadows raced passed her bedroom window. She peeled back the sheets and tumbled onto her feet in jerky motion. The head rush set in, as her blood pressure dropped. Momentary blurred vision obscured her eyeshot to the side yard. Whispered voices outside landed like knocks against the windowpane. Once her eyes adjusted to the dark, she saw the honeysuckle shrub nestled on the neighbor's lattice fence. Suddenly dusky shapes stepped in front of the orange flower petals. Mrs. Quirke scrambled back to the bedside table, back to the gun.

Armed with the revolver, she pointed the barrel past the glass pane. Whatever was there before had left. She waited for a glimpse of movement until hushed laughter came from out of view. She ran to the back door. At the window, she placed a hand over her brow for a better look. "Get off my property," she said. "I have a gun." She flipped the switch on her flood lights. "Don't make me shoot."

Figures gamboled into the shade of night. She raised the barrel to her eyeline and aligned the sights. One shadow stood in place, as the others leapt over the fence and fled. She took aim on the still one. Her index finger hooked the trigger. She exhaled. An outline of the person's head lined up with the muzzle. She fired.

The stranger toppled into a bed of poppies at the foot of her flowering dogwood. She got him. Her braced shoulders went slack. She walked into the yard. Her bare feet glided on blades of grass. Underneath the tree lay the nymph figurine. The head shattered at the neck and left face down in the flowerbed. Mrs. Quirke dropped the gun on the ground. She took notice of the offscourings around her. Rolls of toilet paper cascaded from the branches above. Cracked shells and egg yolk coated the deck. She fell to her knees. The turf abraded her kneecaps as she crawled, on all fours, toward the severed pate. She ferreted in the buffalo grass until she found the fractured plaster piece. She sniveled. Her lips quivered—the nymph's crown cradled in the palm of her hand. Tears flooded her flushed cheeks. As she wept, the titters of children echoed down the street.

Mrs. Quirke's strides came to a halt at the end of the trail. There, she stood at an overlook and leaned toward the creek. Early morning rain fed into the freshet. The intersecting streams met at the diverge she stood upon. She listened to the distant hoot of a mourning dove. Her eyes drifted from the creek to discover a new Media Wars label stuck to the utility pole. She turned away, popped headphones in and clicked play on a podcast. She ran back the way she came. Hasty footfalls carried her home.

WOLF SKIN

by Oliver Fosten

Content Warning: Mentions of Abuse, Slut-Shaming

The path was too clearly marked by the wear of feet and wheels for anyone with sense to lose their way. Even then, the forest was gentle enough that, so long as one made sure to whistle or sing to themself, they could forage or gather kindling in peace. It was only once the moon rose that the accord between human and nature dissolved, and anything could happen if one or both parties hungered enough. Even outlaws knew better than to frequent the woods once twilight fell.

And knowing all this like she knew her own name, she left the path behind her, waiting for something to find her that knew even a hint of mercy. The grip around her basket could have belonged to a marble statue. Her decision was made, but her body only knew the risks that came with spilling the cheese, bread, and other offerings grandmother demanded. Now, grandmother could gnash her teeth and thrash about all she pleased. It wouldn't upright the basket or breathe life back into her granddaughter.

Despite being the precursor and successor to every wrenching memory grandmother carved into her, the forest remained a wondrous place. Time flowed differently among the ancient trees. The moss and lichen absorbed excess sound, the call of birds made distant by the height of the branches they bounced between. Fog always crept between the ferns, the thin streams snaking between the trunks whispering amongst themselves. Rotting leaves and rich soil warmed the body upon each inhale, life and death cycling as easily as air through her lungs.

She halted so abruptly that her shoes dug into the soft earth. Golden eyes flashed from the brush, sending her heart racing with a rabbit's fleet even as her body went rigid. She didn't doubt the predator's gaze was locked upon her long before she spotted the beast in turn. While her feet seemed to find every stray twig and crisp leaf, the aromas from her basket weaving their ways through the gnarled trees, the beast moved as lightly as a shadow. As much as she wished it would have struck before dread set in, the ending would be the same.

Unable to shun hard-learned habits, she set the basket down on a flat patch of moss. Scavengers would quickly find it, but she wouldn't be the one to scatter its contents. She unfastened the travel cloak her mother made for her and hung it on the waiting limb of a nearby tree. If anyone ever found it, there would be no doubt who it once belonged to. Grandmother frequently called the vivid color "slatternly," but never threw the garment into the fire as she threatened. Better for her to wear it and let everyone see exactly what she was.

And with those two tasks completed, she sat on the loamy ground, closing her eyes and exposing her throat.

"There's no need to tremble, child. These woods are my domain, and I grant you safe passage."

There was a strange cadence to the words: formal, dated. It brought to mind the flutish tones of girls on the cusp of adolescence, childish lisps giving way to speaking of the world as their mothers and elder sisters did. When she dared face the stranger in front of her, there was only a wolf peering at her with those same golden eyes. Compared to the great wolves she'd seen hunters brag about skinning, this one was hardly larger than the dogs minding the sheep.

Only she could seek out a mindless animal and instead find some sort of fae. Earning the ire of such old magic was a grim fate, even compared to arriving at grandmother's past the expected time.

"Thank you, but the thought of being eaten by you or your kin isn't what frightens me."

The wolf tilted its head. "The only thing at the end of this path is the old woodcutter's cottage where the witch lives."

"She isn't a witch." Was the only thing she could think to reply with.

"You're right, witches are usually helpful. That old woman is merely a spiteful crone." The wolf sat back on its haunches, ready to wait for her to find her rationale. "Again, I ask you why you're so set on this path when nothing good lies at the end of it."

"That spiteful crone is grandmother."

A long moment passed, the wolf almost seeming to nod at the unpleasant twist the conversation had taken, muzzle creasing in distaste.

"So that's why you'd rather take the perilous route through the woods than the shortcut along the road. Now that I think about it, I recall seeing your red cloak from afar. Equally, I remember the smell of blood and tears as you left the cottage."

Her face burned, eyes prickling. As long as nobody else acknowledged it, she could ignore the throbbing welts across her back, the metallic taste that wouldn't leave her mouth. She quit letting her mother tend to her wounds as soon as she learned to dress them herself. Her mother knew exactly what happened at the old woodcutter's cottage, but that didn't mean she had to be forced to stare at the outcome, her matching scars echoing their ache.

"Your grandmother possesses a cruelty even the most voracious monster could never match. I see not why you continue to bring her food, chop firewood, draw water from the river, and perform other such kindnesses she hasn't earned."

"If I don't care for her, nobody else will. My mother can't make the journey any longer."

"And how many journeys to the cottage do you think your own daughter will make until she drifts off the road and into the woods?" The wolf replied, neither tender, nor harsh.

Her breath hitched against the sobs she forced down, eyes furiously blinking away the beading moisture. If she lost control of herself now, she wouldn't be able to stop. The wolf approached her, butting its head against her shoulder, cold nose tickling her neck. She wrapped her arms around its solid frame, fingers sinking into coarse fur. How strange it was to be embracing a wolf as the moon began its climb overhead, owls calling out as even the last creatures to seek shelter for the night were drifting away into their dreams. She was due at the cottage hours ago, grandmother's fury over the tardiness likely eclipsed by the raging notion she would be left without fresh rations for several days, the time in which her courier was expected home and would be missed.

"Better me than anyone else," She murmured, the words having been repeated to the point where they no longer held any meaning.

"Why is that?"

"I share her blood."

The wolf huffed. "I see not how that matters. Bitterness will keep her alive long after you and the rest of your bloodline are gone. There will always be somebody else given to her."

"Then what choice is there?"

"There is always a choice, child. You found one when you left the path this evening. I present to you a different one. She will steal the very life from you as she did your mother before you if you allow it, just as she will until the end of time."

"You said grandmother isn't a witch. She has to die eventually."

"Of course," The wolf replied. "And then someone else will take her place. There will always be hags and incubi and all manners of monsters both real and fictitious. In turn, there must always be guardians. That cottage holds a long and abominable history. Whatever comes to take your grandmother's place will thirst for the same sacrifices. No one can ever stop wickedness as a whole, but they can burn away the tendrils it reaches out with before it ensnares innocents."

The realization of what the wolf was implying made her breath leave her like a hiss of steam, water thrown over barely kindled embers.

"I don't have the strength or courage to do what you're suggesting."

"Perhaps not, but you can obtain it." The wolf turned its large head towards where she left her cloak and provisions. "Take the knife from your basket and cut away my skin, then your own. I will don yours, and you mine. You will lack neither strength nor courage when you are armored with a thick coat and wield pointed teeth. There will be nothing stopping you from cleansing the woodcutter's cottage and leaving even the most vile of things hesitant to claim it."

"And what then?"

"These woods aren't cursed. They readily nourish those who care for it in turn. Follow the path of the wolf and learn to see the beauty in the world again. In time, when you have healed, you will don human skin once again and return to what you left behind. That is what I did, and will do."

"What is your story?"

"One not too different from yours, child. When my father remarried, his new wife had no desire to compete for his attention with another woman, even if said woman was but a child. He told my elder brother to leave me in the heart of these woods. By the time I realized what was happening, he'd left me and picked up the trail of stones he made so I couldn't follow him home. The wolf I met in these woods was a young woman who fled for her life when she found a room of blood and corpses her husband locked away. She licked the tears from my face and assured me the woods would never turn away from me as my kin had, would shelter me for as long as I needed as I learned to carry the hurt dealt to me."

"So I'm to rip my grandmother apart with teeth and claws."

"How you use your new form is up to you. My predecessor howled until the stone of her husband's castle came crashing down, entombing him with the women he was so desperate to possess. I brought the horror of the woods to dog my family's every step. My brother spent his life repenting his sins in the clergy. My father took his ax to the woman who poisoned his mind against his own child, and then a rope to himself for allowing the festering to consume his family. The only regret I have is not letting the forest take the cottage. How you decide to repay the debts your grandmother has forced onto you is your choice."

So she stood, dusting the debris from her stockings and skirts, and retrieved the knife from the basket.

Even before she felt the way the breeze ruffled her fur, how her center of gravity shifted to accommodate four sturdy legs, massive maw, and a bushy tail, she knew there had been a change. Several colors she knew tinted the leaves and fat berry bushes were now muddy shades of brown and gray. More surprising was how sharply she could see the woods around her given how brightly the stars still shone against the black velvet sky. The instinctive knowledge from the musk in the air that a rabbit warren lay buried nearby set her nose twitching, saliva flooding her mouth. Boughs creaked, vermin scurried through the underbrush, and other night creatures rose to begin their rounds.

Despite how far she'd wandered from the trail when she still walked on two legs, there was no difficulty in reorienting herself. She caught the scent of the cottage's wood stove and aging flesh, loping between the trees with unmatched endurance and swiftness, her cloak a streaming banner held between clenched teeth. Her hackles stood on end as the trees thinned, giving way to a clearing. A few tattered ribbons swayed from the boughs, wards to keep the evil eye contained or proof some daring youth dared creep so close to the maligned cottage.

In another's hands, the cottage might have been a charming thing. It was only one room, a bed in one corner and a table, stove, and cabinet in the others. There weren't any colorful baubles, or even a simple jar of flowers to lessen the austerity. The bed wasn't any more comfortable than the floor, though it was slightly warmer underneath the scratchy blankets. Stone walls sagged in random directions, the thatching on the roof rotting at the edges. The jagged teeth of the fence enclosed it all, weeds peppering the dusty ground. If any joy went into the building of the cottage, it fled soon afterward.

It took her a long moment to remember how to use her human voice, but it rang through her ears just as it had in her old body. "Grandmother!"

Behind the cottage walls, the chair groaned. Stockinged feet scraped against the rough floorboards until grandmother found her wooden shoes, then the rod kept in the corner. The door barked against the end of its hinges as grandmother stormed out to drag her inside and beat an explanation for her tardiness out of her, letting the welts rise so the next strikes would sting more. They didn't end until the rod broke or grandmother's bones ached too much to continue.

But all grandmother saw in the clearing before the cottage was a wolf hardly out of its whelp phase, a wadded up cloak at its feet. The brilliant color of the cloak was now lost to the wolf, but not grandmother. She looked between the cloak and the wolf, expression cycling between confusion, realization, and finally, fear.

She was no longer some quivering girl for grandmother to savage, but a creature capable of destruction in her own right. A victim could be trusted to remain meek, docile. An opponent would assure only one of them would leave the cottage. The rod couldn't hurt her any longer, about as useful against a wolf as tickling it. If she possessed any final hesitations, they were obliterated when grandmother's eyes turned to the poker and its twin points beside the fireplace.

All the muscles in her new body bunched and sprang as she leapt. The momentum knocked grandmother back like an oncoming wave, nails tearing weeping holes in her nightgown as her spectacles went skittering across the floor. Breathless, grandmother kicked and gauged at her newly lupine face with withered talons. Raw, animal rage that had been left to simmer finally boiled over. No one would scar this beautiful new skin of hers. Certainly not scar her and live, and they both knew it.

"I-"

Whatever curse grandmother was preparing to spew at her was drowned out in a gurgle, blood arcing through the air as her throat was torn out between the wolf's righteous jaws. When the sputtering gasps halted, the wolf sat back, using her tongue to clean away the gore spattered over her silver coat, letting it slip down her throat like the sweetest of wine. Once finished, she lifted her head to the night sky and sang.

How long had it been since she traded away her human skin? A year? A decade? A century? The shoes that swaddled her feet may have protected her from cuts and calluses, but they also dulled her ability to feel the swells and dips of the ground, leaving her stumbling over each minor change in terrain. Without her shaggy coat to protect her, the chill burrowed underneath her skin even as the urge to tear away the stockings, gloves, undergarments that were chafing at her left her snarling. The sound emerged pitchy and aborted, her vocal chords no longer able to produce the rumble she was reaching for. Aside from her own footsteps and the occasional rustle of leaves from some small animal, which her nose could no longer place as easily as if she saw it in front of her, silence surrounded her. The shadows were too dark, the beams of light that wormed their way through the boughs blinding as the sun rose ever higher.

She readily took to living as a wolf, running through the trees until she collapsed in a panting heap, bloodying her entire face in her kills, howling simply to hear her cries echo around her, sometimes returned by other wolves who perhaps also knew far too much about humanity. For the first time she could recall, hunger wasn't gnawing at her inside, she possessed the energy, the freedom, to romp and play and be the child she was. It was only when the vulnerable started along the forest path that she remembered herself and took to minding the strangers, ensuring they safely arrived at their destination. There had only been a few times when she'd been forced to intervene, but a snarl and gnash of the teeth was always enough to keep foolish children going in the correct direction or scare away those with wicked intentions. Today, though, was the first time she spoke to one of the travelers.

She could only blink as she stepped beyond the treeline, the world she turned her back on now laid out before her. A milestone rested not far down the road, worn smooth from the elements and countless bodies resting against its cool face before trudging onward. Smoke curled into the air not far beyond the hills from a smattering of chimneys. It was as good a place to begin again as any. The path she was on would eventually lead from the woods to the hamlet to a city. Each stop, each choice, would be hers to make.

I HEAR YOU

by Katie Kent

Content Warning: Homophobia, Bullying

Dear Joey,

I've wanted to write this letter for a while now. I like everything about you, from the copper tinge of your hair to your beautiful green eyes, to the way your face lights up when you read your poetry in English. When I see you, it's like nothing else matters. Like if I looked up 'perfection' in the dictionary, there would just be a photo of you.

I've been scared to tell you how I feel, because there's a big chance you don't feel the same way. I haven't seen you with a girl, but then I haven't seen you with a boy, either. I know statistically you're more likely to be straight. But as long as there is a chance, I have to say something.

I'm banking on you being a nice person. I'm banking on you letting me down gently, if you don't feel the same way. If you're not into girls like that, I will be disappointed, of course. But I will deal with it. I just have to find out. My hands are shaking as I write this, but at least I'll soon know, one way or the other.

Yours,

Madison.

"If I looked up 'perfection' in the dictionary, there would just be a photo of you."

Laughter breaks out amongst the assembled crowd.

"Honestly, Maddie, where did you get this shit from? I can't believe you honestly thought I might be into girls."

I count to ten in my head as I face the girl who, until a few minutes ago, I thought was the most amazing one in the universe. My opinion of her plummeted as soon as she started reading my letter out loud. The letter I had written for her eyes only. At least now I know. I know she isn't into me. I know she's straight. And I know she's an asshole.

"Screw you." I don't know what else to say. She's not only broken my heart; she's torn it into thousands of tiny little pieces.

She shrugs. "I know you'd like to. You made that perfectly clear in that pathetic attempt at a love letter."

I feel my face turn red as the other kids giggle around me. One of them wolf-whistles. The thing I hate the most is that when I look at her, my body still reacts in the way it has for months. I still can't take my eyes off her face. I still can't stop imagining what it would be like to run my fingers through her hair, to feel her lips on mine, to walk hand-in-hand with her through the corridors.

"I can't believe I never noticed you undressing me with your eyes before," she says.

"I can't believe I never realized what a bitch you are before." The thought is out of my mouth before I can stop it, but I mean every word.

The smile slips from her face for just a moment, but she composes herself quickly. The bell rings for the next class, and the other kids reluctantly disperse until it's just the two of us standing there, face-to-face. She licks her lips and I fold my arms, knowing she's teasing me and wanting to show I don't care, even though I do.

"See you later." She winks at me, tosses her hair over her shoulder, and walks off, leaving me standing there alone.

I shake my head as I walk to my next class.

"I'm sorry that happened to you," my best friend, Kate, says when I tell her. "She's a bitch. Want me to beat her up for you?"

Despite everything, I smile. Kate is tiny—she wouldn't have a chance against Joey. "Thanks, but I'll be okay."

"Alright." She puts her hand on my arm. "But let's hang out after school, yeah? I'll buy you a chocolate milkshake."

"That would be nice, thanks."

I put myself out there and Joey not only shot me down, she trampled all over my feelings. My tactic going forward will be to ignore her as much as possible. Hopefully this, in conjunction with the fact I now know what a horrible person she is, will help my crush end soon. Although past evidence is not very encouraging. It took ages for my crush on Kate to fade into something more manageable, even though I knew she was straight.

"Thanks for this," I say, as we sit opposite each other at the diner later. A storm is brewing outside, and the gray sky matches my mood.

Kate's smile takes my mind off Joey for just a second. "What are friends for? You know I've got your back."

I briefly wish it was still her I was into. At least I know she wouldn't have publicly humiliated me like Joey did. But it surely would have put an end to our friendship, and that was the reason I forced myself to get over my thing for her. Now there are two girls I've spent months pining over to no avail and I wonder if any girl will ever like me the way I like her. The thought causes a sigh to travel the whole length of my body, and Kate's eyes fill with compassion.

"Hey, what you did was really brave. You just need better taste." She gives me a playful wink, and I can't help laughing.

"Oh yeah? Like who?"

"I dunno. Someone less of a bitch, obviously. And someone less straight."

I roll my eyes. "No shit."

She picks up a french fry and tosses it at me.

"Hey!" I wipe the splatter of ketchup from my nose.

The rumble of thunder in the distance makes us both look out the window.

Kate pulls a face. "It's getting bleak out there."

Just as I'm taking a sip of my milkshake, a boy I recognise from school, but whose name I don't remember, approaches our table.

"Hey, just so you know," he addresses Kate, "people are talking. You know, because you're friends with *her*. You'd be better off finding someone else to hang out with."

My heart sinks, but Kate wasn't lying when she said she had my back.

"Maybe you're the one who should look for new friends," she tells him. "Sounds like your current ones are bigoted."

"Maybe he's right," I say, once he's left our table. I suddenly become aware of the looks and giggles from the group he's part of. "Perhaps we should avoid hanging out for a while. You know, until this has all died down. It's bad enough how they're treating me. I don't want you to have to put up with this too."

She just shrugs. "We're best friends, right? We don't abandon each other when things get tough. Anyway, I'd kind of miss you."

I don't say anything, just reach out and give her hand a quick squeeze. A bolt of lightning flashes right by the window we're sitting at, and we drop each other's hands at the exact same moment.

"Ouch," she says, shaking hers. "Electric shock."

I flex my fingers, watching the rain start to come down. "Well, I guess we're here for a while."

"Maddie, it's time to get up."

I groan as I rub the sleep out of my eyes. I'd been in the middle of a full-on romantic dream about me and Joey, and I'd just got to the bit where we were about to kiss.

Why does she look so sad all the time?

"I'm fine," I say, but Mom just narrows her eyes. "I never said you weren't."

"But..." As I look at her, I realize I didn't see her mouth move when I heard her say I looked sad. And she framed it in the third person.

I wish she'd tell me what's going on. Is this my fault? I have to bite my tongue to stop from telling Mom that no, of course it's not her fault. She smiles at me. "Shall I make you some breakfast?"

"I'm not hungry." My stomach is churning.

She looks thin. Should I ring the doctor?

I have no idea why I can suddenly hear Mom's thoughts, but I don't want her thinking I'm anorexic or anything. I sigh. "Alright, I could manage a couple of pieces of toast."

She beams, putting her hand on my arm briefly before leaving the room.

After she's gone, I let out a breath. What's happening to me? I haven't got time to think about it too much, though—I've got to get to school.

I get dressed and pack my things, then head downstairs. I shove the toast into my mouth and chew, trying to avoid Mom's thoughts, but they echo around me. She's thinking about me and whether I'm doing okay, her upcoming day at work, and her handsome, married, boss. Eew. That's something I'd rather not know.

I almost choke on my toast in my haste to leave, which worries Mom even more. I hadn't realized she was such a worrier. Suddenly I panic that she might be able to hear my thoughts, too.

Mom, can you hear me? I think, but she gives no indication she can.

"See you later." I give her a kiss on the cheek and open the front door, relieved to be away from her thoughts.

I usually listen to a podcast on the way to school, but today I walk in silence.

Jealousy stabs me as I see a girl about my age walking hand-in-hand with a boy up ahead.

Lisa is so freaking hot.

I sigh, wishing someone would think about me that way.

I know Helen will hate me, but I'm gonna have to break up with her tonight. I know Lisa wants me.

I suddenly come to a stop, letting them get out of my eyesight. Whatever this strange ability is that I've suddenly developed, it seems more like a curse. I don't want to know what other people are thinking. It was bad enough when it was just Mom. For the rest of the walk, I cross the road every time I see someone. It probably looks really odd, but it's better than hearing all these thoughts now being beamed into my head.

When I'm almost at school, my phone buzzes with a text from Kate. She's got a migraine and won't be in today. I'm actually kind of relieved, to be honest. Hearing my best friend's thoughts would feel like a bit of an intrusion. What if she thought I was being annoying or something? She and Mom are all I have now.

If I thought the walk to school was bad, arriving at school is worse.

Seven hours to go. I hate kids.

My jaw drops as I pass Mr Benson. He always looks so cheerful. Indeed, he gives me a cheery wave as I pass.

What will they find about me to take the piss out of today? My parents will kill me if I didn't pass that test. Should I ask him out? I wish I'd just drop dead. I can't believe Madison wrote that letter, what a loser! If only I had the guts to do what Madison did.

I clap my hands over my ears, trying to shut it all out. My heart is racing. If anyone could hear *my* thoughts right now, they'd hear: *I must be going crazy. What's happening to me? How do I make this stop?*

I'm on the verge of walking out of school—and I've never missed a day in my life—until I hear another thought that stops me in my tracks.

Oh God, it's Madison. Quick, look away. Joey sneers at me as she walks past.

I just stare at her back as she walks away.

*Did she buy that? They'll get suspicious if I'm nice to her. Maybe I shouldn't have read her letter out loud. But I couldn't let her know...*she steps into the toilets, and I can't hear her anymore.

I lean back against the wall, suddenly exhausted. I can still hear thoughts all around me, but I don't pay attention to them. So she likes me after all. The knowledge should make me happy, but I really don't know what to do with it. It's clear she is firmly in the closet and has every intention of staying that way.

I absent-mindedly twirl my hair around my finger. The door opens, and Joey steps back out.

God, does she have to keep doing that? If only I could kiss her. Shut up, Joey. She'll notice. Just act cool. Act like you can't stand her. "Quit staring at me, would you? I told you, I'm not into you. You're just embarrassing yourself." *I wish I didn't have to be so mean to her.* I don't even know what to say to her, so I don't say anything. I just turn my back on her and walk away.

After homeroom, Joey and I share English class together. I take the seat opposite her and make a show of twirling my hair slowly around my finger whilst looking down at my exercise book. I have to admit, it's kind of fun knowing the effect I'm having on her.

I want her so bad it hurts. It's worse now I know she likes me too. How do I get her out of my head? I can hear the thoughts of the other kids too and it's still pretty overwhelming, but Joey's thoughts rise above all the others. Despite enjoying my ability to do this to her, I feel sorry for her at the same time.

"Who knows what a haiku is?" Miss James asks.

Joey's hand shoots up.

"Yes, Joey?"

"It's a poem with three lines," she says. "The first and last lines have five syllables, and the second has seven."

"Exactly." Miss James smiles at her, and then reads an example from her book. "Now, let's have a stab at writing some."

The class goes quiet— not for me, of course. I can hear thoughts all around me. Some kids are thinking about the exercise, but others are thinking about what they're going to have for dinner later, or who they fancy. One boy is even fantasizing about Miss James.

I look at Joey's head bent over her exercise book, her pen poised on the paper.

I want her so bad.

But no one can know my thoughts.

How do I hide this?

I tap my pen against the desk. Next to me, Ben looks up and glares I stop the tapping and whisper, "Sorry."

Another kid whose name I don't even remember looks at me, then at Joey, and smirks.

I can't believe Joey's even writing haikus about me. She must have it bad.

I force myself to concentrate on the exercise. I'm tempted to write a haiku about her, but even though everyone now knows how I feel, I can't read that out if Miss James picks on me. I know it would embarrass Joey, as well as myself. So I write something bland about the weather.

"Time's up. Now, who wants to read theirs out?"

No one puts their hand up. Miss James frowns. "I can't believe you're all so shy. Joey, why don't you go first?"

Joey clears her throat, and I hold my breath.

"Leaves fall from the trees.

I kick them under my feet.

It's the start of Fall."

I let my breath out, feeling slightly deflated. Of course she wasn't going to read a haiku about me out to the class.

When the bell goes for the end of the school day, I race out of there. Hearing everyone's thoughts has given me a headache, and I feel like I need to lie down in a quiet room for a bit. Luckily, Mom will be at work for the next couple of hours, so I won't have to deal with her thoughts straight away.

I keep my head down as I walk home, trying to ignore the thoughts of everyone who walks past. When I get to my house, it seems so quiet. I go up to my room and lay on my bed, but I can't relax enough to sleep. I know Joey likes me, but she seems so scared of her sexuality. So what can I do about it? If I confront her, she'll just deny it, and I can hardly tell her I've heard her thoughts. I groan into my pillow. This ability has not helped me, it's just made things worse.

I try to distract myself by texting Kate. 'Feeling any better? x'.

She texts back immediately. 'Yeah, a bit. How was school? Sorry I wasn't there to back you up against evil Joey x'.

I chuckle. 'It was fine.' My finger hesitates over the touchscreen. I want to tell her about my ability, about the fact that I know Joey is as into me as I am into her, but I don't want Kate thinking I've gone mad. 'Don't worry about me x.'

I set my alarm early the next morning and leave Mom a scribbled note to say I've decided to go in early to get in some extra study time. Last night was as bad as this morning. No one needs to hear their mom fantasizing about all the things they'd like to do to their boss.

I was hoping it was just a 24-hour thing, but I can still hear the thoughts of people who pass me on the way to school and my heart sinks. What if I'm like this for the rest of my life? What if I hear someone thinking about a crime they've committed, or something?

Joey winks at me again and the kids stood near to her snigger. *They have to think this is all a big joke to me.*

As if Madison would have a chance with someone like Joey, one of the boys thinks. Although... it would be hot to watch.

I shake my head.

"Hey. I got you something."

I turn around to see Kate and immediately sweep her into a hug.

"Careful," she says. "You'll crush your brownie."

She hands me a paper bag and I pull it out. It's a mint choc chip–my favorite. I always feel better when Kate's around. She always knows how to cheer me up. I just hope her thoughts don't reveal anything too private.

When we pull apart she looks at Joey and suddenly her eyes go wide.

Holy shit, she's into Maddie? Joey is gay?

My mouth hangs open. There's no way Kate could know. Unless...

Can you hear me, Kate?

She swallows. "Uh, I gotta pee."

She flees, leaving me standing there confused. The knowledge that I'm not the only one comforts me, but why is she acting so weird?

I walk into the toilets and knock on the door of the only occupied stall. "Kate?"

"Leave me alone," she says. *Don't let her hear you.*

"What's going on?" I ask, gently.

Polar bear, fire engine, pink elephant. La la la.

What are you doing? I know she can hear my thoughts. *What are you trying to hide from me?*

*Think about anything but how much you love her.
Oh shit. Shit shit shit shit shit.*

You love me?!

Shit. I told you to leave me alone. Look what you've done.

"Why didn't you tell me?" I take a step closer to the door, trying to close the distance between us. I'd thought I knew everything about Kate. We've been friends since we were little kids. I'd been honest with her about my sexuality, but she never let me suspect she was anything other than straight.

I'm bi.

I sigh. "Kate, we need to talk about this. Like, properly talk. Not just listen to each other's thoughts."

The door clicks open. Kate faces me, her cheeks red. "I never wanted you to find out."

"Why not?" I ask, quietly.

She shrugs. "You're into Joey." *I hate her. I want to stick my fingers in her eyes and pull her hair out.*

I try to suppress a smile. "I never thought you were an option."

It's true Joey has occupied my thoughts for the last few months. But now I let myself think about last year—the many months I spent fantasizing about Kate being my girlfriend. I didn't want to ruin our friendship, so when Joey came along and I felt an attraction to her, I let myself fixate on her to dampen what I felt for Kate. And it worked, to an extent.

She's so close I only need to lean forward slightly and our lips would be touching. She must hear that thought, as a smile flickers across her face.

She chews her thumbnail. "But Joey likes you back. How can I compete with that?"

"She's never going to admit it," I say. "She doesn't want anyone to know she's gay." I look into Kate's brown eyes, at her long, brown hair, those old feelings starting to come back. "What about you?"

"I'm not scared of anyone finding out. I just wanted to hide it from you, because I thought you weren't interested and I didn't want to ruin what we had as friends."

My heart hammers in my chest. *Maybe you could kiss me now.*

She smiles. "That can be arranged." She tilts her face towards mine and then I'm tasting her vanilla lip gloss. Her lips are soft and warm, and for a moment, she is all I think about.

The bathroom door swings open.

OH MY GOD. What the hell are they doing? God, stop staring.

Kate and I pull apart at the same moment.

"That's disgusting." Joey's bottom lip curls up.

Kate and I look at each other and burst out laughing. I hold my side; I haven't laughed this much in ages.

"Are you sure you wouldn't rather be with her?" Kate's face goes serious as Joey flees the bathroom.

I link my fingers with hers. *I want you, Kate.*

She grins. "I don't know how we developed these abilities, but without it this would never have happened." She pauses. "I hope it goes soon, though. I could do without knowing every time you find another girl cute."

I lean forward to push a lock of hair out of her face.

God, she's gorgeous.

I smirk. "I dunno, I could get used to hearing you think about how much you like me."

ISOLATION TRAINING

by Gwen Tolios

Jenji stared at her next challenge.

While she knew the structure was a training capsule, stocked with non-perishable food and equipped with a space-caliber water recycling system, in her head she thought of it as a boxcar. There were no windows, only a large door on one end. It sat in a large cement room, surrounded by video monitors connected to the cameras in the capsule. Come tomorrow afternoon, this *box* would be her home for the next six weeks.

She wasn't looking forward to it.

When she had been evaluated for the astronaut program, years ago, she'd been bombarded with questions. What she thought her strengths were, her weaknesses, her fears. She'd lied about the last one, telling a story about how as a child she'd slipped off a rocky outcropping, fell into the ocean, and panicked for three seconds before scrambling back onto the rocks.

The memory, she told the man across from her, had instilled a strong fear of deep water in her.

Jenji thought it was a good fake fear — there's no ocean in space. It also allowed her to show herself overcoming adversity, "working through her fear" until she was comfortable with the underwater training designed to mimic the vacuum of space as much as possible on Earth. Who knows, maybe her acting had been the extra push that resulted in her selection as a crew member for three missions. It might have been cheating the system, but NASA was very, very selective. She'd do anything for an edge.

This next mission though, a chance to *set foot on Mars,* pitted her against her actual fear. Isolation.

A yet-to-be-picked astronaut would ride a rocket into space to play truck driver delivering three years of supplies to the Mars colony and then turn around and come back. They would be traveling solo both ways for a total of nineteen months.

Jenji had never been in space longer than six, and she'd never been alone more than an extended weekend.

Make no mistake, Mars was her dream. To step on the red planet and see her boot print in the soil. To look up at Earth and see it not as a blue-and-white orb, but a speck of light in the sky. Spend time on another world, full of things to explore. Still, the idea of spending more than a-year-and-a-half alone, being away from Casper for so long...

She'd developed a recurring nightmare. She'd be in a small, wooden rowboat with peeling gray paint. It'd rock with the swells of the ocean, and the only sound she heard was the click of her own tongue against the roof of her mouth. No splashes. No birds. No fish bubbles or far-off fog horns.

When she looked over the side of the boat, the water turned to ink and stars bloomed around her. The boat grew walls until it transformed into the capsule she'd spend the trip in. With the switch in vessels, her pulse skyrocketed as fear filled the tight space. When she opened her mouth to scream, she often woke up, mouth in real life also open but silent.

In space, no one can hear you scream. The tagline for *Alien* had sent a delightful thrill of horror-fun down her spine at age thirteen. At thirty-six, the line's stark truth downright terrified her.

She'd wake gasping and sweaty, jackknifing upright in bed, and immediately turn to Casper's sleeping form, praying they didn't wake up. Sometimes they did, sometimes they didn't, but regardless, Jenji would scoot closer and curl up as tight as she could against her spouse's body. The dreams were silly, she wasn't claustrophobic, and Casper's soothing breaths lulled Jenji back to sleep.

As a couple, they'd talked about Jenji's departures into space. Together, they knew how to calm nerves, weather the anxiety, when to talk about a nightmare and when not to. Casper said their piece years ago, expressing their worry and fear about Jenji's career even as she tried to explain the lure of the stars and the way her body lit up when strapped to rocket fuel.

Care. Comfort. Support. It got them through seven years of dating, five years of marriage, and two of Jenji's three missions into space. It would get her through this one too.

Alone, alone, alone.

NASA had found a strong correlation between an astronaut's ability to survive six weeks in isolation with their ability to handle the mental strain of solo missions over six months.

You can do this, Jenji. Some alone time will be good for you. Besides, if you don't pass this test, you'll be removed from the shortlist of astronauts being considered for the mission.

Jenji hugged herself and stared at the large box from across the room. Tomorrow, she'd step inside and be locked in. She raised both hands and flicked the training capsule off, trying to hide her fear, but she wasn't sure it worked.

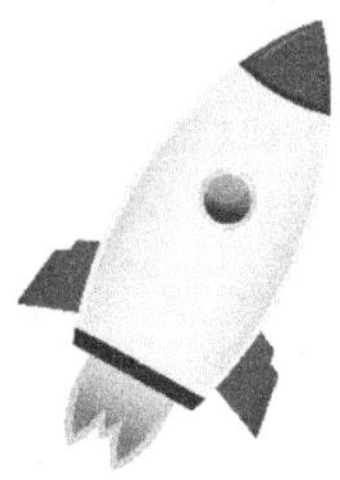

"All set, Stevenson?" Nico asked as another lab tech did one final check of the supplies in the capsule. Both of them were on the team monitoring her time in the training capsule.

"All set," Jenji replied. She hitched up her child-sized backpack. Cargo space was a hot commodity in space and personal items were kept to a minimum. Jenji had packed things she hoped would replace the dozens of people she'd usually surround herself with.

Or at least, keep her too occupied to remember she was alone.

"In you go, then," Nico said, gesturing to the open door.

Strutting aboard, Jenji kept up the mantra of *alone is fine, alone is fine, alone is fine.*

She extended her arms in the narrow space and her fingertips pressed against both walls. Thankfully the box-like space was long, eighteen feet according to the specs. The far end contained a small two-person booth whereas behind Jenji loomed a heavy metal door.

"See you in six weeks," Nico said.

Jenji smiled at him and waved, suppressing her panic as the door closed between them. "It'll feel like six days."

A-LONE, the door said as it closed and locked.

Jenji took several deep breaths. Her response to the confinement would be recorded and analyzed. Every expression, every gesture, had the power to cement or destroy her selection for this mission. Jenji couldn't risk that. This might be her only chance to get to Mars.

She set about familiarizing herself with her surroundings. While not an accurate mockup of the final shuttle, the box mimicked it. Various instruments filled most of the left wall. The dials and knobs were labeled with acronyms, but Jenji knew what they all stood for from hours of poring over manuals. Air mixture, fuel, oxygen levels, internal temperature, gyroscopes, and compasses to be used when close to a planet or other object with gravity. Light switches, comm switches, levels to lower shields.

The right wall contained tight living quarters, not quite what she'd have in space because some setups worked better in zero-G, but there was a set of tight bunk beds, the bottom one containing a sleeping bag that in space would be strapped to a wall. She barely fit in the shower, and thankfully a gravity-powered Earth toilet and not a suction-powered space one was behind a curtain away from the cameras. Her kitchen, at the end of the wall, contained only a microwave and hot plate.

At least the small nook at the end, with an L-shaped booth and table that slid in and out of the right wall, looked comfortable to sit in.

It'll be like a camping trip, she told herself, *in a really tight RV with no car attached.*

She conducted a slow, thorough investigation of the training capsule's items. Rubbed her sleeping bag between two fingers. Fiddled with the non-working dials and switches. Sat at the table, pleased to find sitting in the middle of the bench gave her elbow room on both sides. Explored and identified the materials in every storage compartment. Most of it was food: canned veggies and pasta. This training wasn't supposed to accurately mimic space living, it was focused on judging psychological stability, so she was spared the freeze-dried food. There were reminders to adhere to serving sizes taped to the inside of the food cabinets. It wouldn't do to run out of pasta three days early because she made bigger bowls than needed.

To that extent, she made sure when making dinner to level off the measuring cup to ensure she didn't use too much.

She finished dinner at seven-thirty. Shortly afterward, the loneliness crept in.

Why did her first night in this box have to be a Tuesday?

She and Casper liked catching happy hours or shows in the city, an occasional dinner with friends, but Tuesdays were "couple nights." Quiet nights, spent solely with each other.

Jenji itched for Casper's radiant heat. To lean into their shoulder while the two of them watched TV. The rhythm of their baritone voice as they talked about their day and plans for the week. Or the smoothness of their freshly shaved legs brushing hers under a blanket. She wanted to call them, but she had no means to do so. She wanted to pretend they were there and talk out loud, but worried how that would look on camera.

*You have to show you can handle it, the soloness, the loneliness. Going to Mars **will** be easy. Not having someone to talk to will **not** drive you crazy.*

She pulled out her tablet. Tried to read. The silence of the box got thicker and thicker. Just for noise, she plugged her flash drive into the computer and played her favorite movie soundtracks. Still, her attention kept straying. She imagined Casper's strong biceps around her, their favorite terry cloth robe soft against her skin and long hair brushing her chin.

Jenji looked at her watch. 9:30 pm. Early, but not an alarmingly early bedtime. She snapped her device closed and got ready for bed. At 9:45, she flipped off the light and crawled into her sleeping bag. The fabric she found smooth as silk earlier now felt like cold water on her feet and she regretted her lack of socks.

It'd be too weird to turn on the lights again just to grab a pair, right? No, no. People got cold feet all the time. Getting socks is a normal thing to do.

She stumbled around in the dark anyway to find socks. Back in her sleeping bag, she turned onto her right side. It felt awkward. She usually slept on her left, nestled in Casper's arms, but this way, the glow of the fake command center filled her vision and reminded her why she was doing this.

If you can last these measly six weeks, you can last to Mars and back.

"I can do this," she mouthed to herself as she fell asleep.

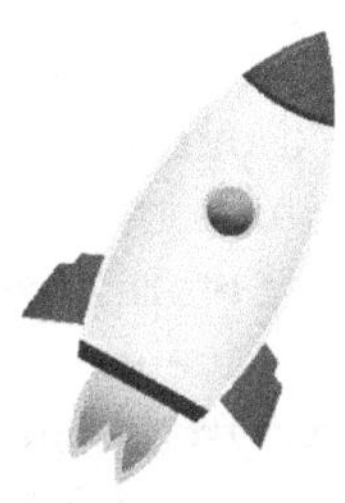

She started her day with actions she hoped to turn into a morning routine. Wake up. Sit-ups. Push-ups. Jumping jacks. When she noticed how little time had passed, she made it longer: bicycles, sit-ups with a twist, knee push-ups, planks, high knees, tricep dips from the floor and the kitchen table, arm circles, and supermans. A second look at her watch showed her routine failed to eat up as much time as she wanted it to, so she slipped into the various yoga stretches she picked up over the years. Not all of them were practical in the strip of open floor between the bunks/shower/toilet and instrument wall, but she made do.

Isolation was a problem NASA had been struggling with for decades and developed procedures to counteract it: daily communication packets to astronauts, detailed itineraries, voice-activated programming, and robots. But Jenji didn't have them, that was the point. She would have to go back to the basics and set up a routine. Keep moving, develop patterns, stay occupied.

Her workout took up the majority of an hour, her quick shower another fifteen minutes, and cooking breakfast another thirty.

Slipping off her watch so she wouldn't look at it constantly, Jenji pulled out her brand new cross-stitch and sat at the table. She took her time, setting out all her colors of thread before creating the necessary combos. Two strands lavender, one strand eggshell white. One strand forest green, one strand charcoal.

It took her longer than expected to prepare her workspace, but she didn't mind. She needed to do things that made time pass quickly. Keeping busy meant she had less time to go crazy.

Her cross-stitch preparations lasted her to lunch. She drew out lunch itself, then started on her pattern - a complicated replication of a Thomas Kincaid painting. After an hour, she realized she was talking herself through the process. "Top right, bottom left, top right, bottom left."

Alarmed, she looked up at the closest ceiling corner and the camera there. Immediately, she looked back at her work.

Talking to herself already. Damn it. Not even a full 24 hours and she already put her chance at being on the mission in jeopardy. She couldn't afford any sign the isolation was getting to her.

Jenji bit her lip, then hurried over to the instrument wall. While not running an active training program, the computer did have basic functions. Plugging in her flash drive, she selected her favorite pop music. The sound of other people's voices immediately made her shoulders unclench, and if she sang along? Well, that was normal human behavior.

As she sat back down, the cross stitch stared at her. She'd completed a bush, just a single bush. The rest of the four by three-foot canvas awaited, but the desire to pick it up again never materialized.

She didn't want to spend the next few hours looking at small holes and a chart of various symbols, accidentally poking her finger with a dull needle and counting stitches. Jenji didn't want to read the book she started last night either.

Instead, she wanted to be on the teeny-tiny balcony at home. Casper telling her about their day at work through the open door while Jenji breathed in lungful after lungful of dry Texan air.

She berated herself for the thought.

Jenji shouldn't, couldn't, be wishing for something else, even if it was simply Casper. Especially after they had been so supportive, cooking meals and quizzing her daily. As a couple, they worked together to push Jenji to the stars. She *needed* to prove she could handle these weeks of isolation.

Get through this, get through this, get through this, Jenji told herself.

Gritting her teeth, she picked up the cross-stitch and started on a second bush, jabbing the needling through a hole and hitting her forefinger underneath. Grumbling, she sucked on the digit before continuing. This cross-stitch *would* become a part of her routine, no matter how much it grated.

She didn't have much else.

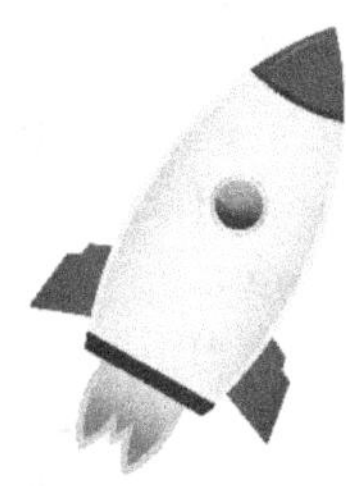

Dinner was lonely. After dinner was lonelier, even if she tried to fake it by cranking up old party tunes and dancing up and down the narrow hallway. For twenty minutes, she lost herself in the movement. The bad speakers in the box made her think of her university haunts. With her eyes closed, she imagined she was moving on a narrow, cramped dance floor.

She forced herself to stay up till 10, then pushed till 10:30, sitting in her sleeping bag while she tried to read the book she'd started earlier. Usually, science fiction thrilled her, but tonight she found the genre held no interest. She wished she'd added a few of Casper's cozy mysteries. They should have made plans like they did on her missions, read the same thing so they could share something while apart, even if the likelihood of Casper finishing a book in six weeks was slim.

Jenji's free time had grown exponentially whereas she knew Casper's would have shrunk due to work or social engagements. They were probably at a bar right now or having dinner with mutual friends, temporarily filling Jenji's space the same way Jenji has used a crewmate's conversation – distractions to alieve the sense of missing someone.

Snapping the tablet closed, she shut off the lights and stared at the ceiling.

Slowly, the noises of the training capsule rose to prominence: the hum of the air conditioning, the slight buzz of the command console.

Jenji knew, objectively, she wasn't alone. There were people outside the training capsule not three meters away, looking at camera feeds. She wasn't in a ship drifting through space, so far away real-time communication was impossible and help would come too late. She wasn't stranded in space, and while she'd faced that fear before it always disappeared as soon as she was strapped to a rocket engine. Once in space, wonder consumed her.

She's always had someone to share that feeling with. Other astronauts on the ISS2. Crewmates on shuttles. There'd be no one to share her wonder with on this mission. No other voice to keep the loneliness at bay. On this mission to Mars, the lack of company would be constant. An inescapable force. Something heavier than the weight currently on her chest.

No help. No escape. She could scream and scream and NASA would never hear.

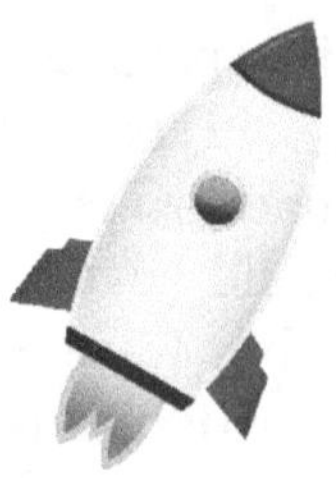

As if taunting her, Jenji's nightmare got worse.

After her small, old grey boat on the sea turned to a capsule amongst the stars, the tiny windows spiraled closed, blocking her view. A background missive from NASA turned to static, then died. Jenji stared at her instruments, prepared to fly and land blind, but they didn't register the presence of Mars. She sat there, hoping for the gravitational readings that would indicate Mars even as food and fuel dwindled.

Eventually, she realized her launch vectors had been wrong. She missed the planet. She didn't know where she was. Communication and rescue was impossible. She'd die of starvation. She slipped into her sleeping bag, hanging upright, and stared at the wall across from her, body going limp as death crept in.

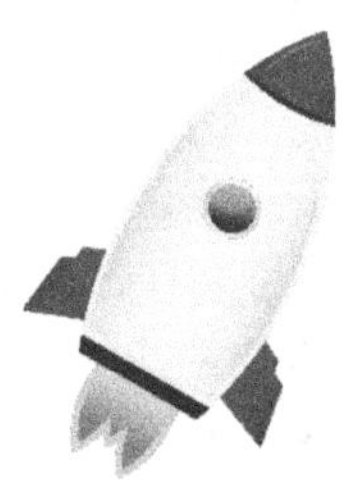

When Jenji opened her eyes, she thought she still dreamed. The view of the bunk above her was identical to the wall in her dream, but the sounds in the background convinced her she was awake. Eager to shake the nightmare off, she slipped out of bed and began her fitness routine.

With every sit-up, she imagined herself forcing open the metal plates across the window. With every bicycle kick, she ran calculations in her head for rations and flight adjustments. As she sunk into warrior pose, she composed messages and pings to send to Mars.

It won't be like that, Jenji told herself. *Every mission NASA has run for the past ten years has been safe. Backups and backups and backups. You're being silly.*

She washed away her worry with her sweat, labelled the dream as a one-off terror. Acknowledge, accept, and place aside.

Jenji was no stranger to compartmentalization.

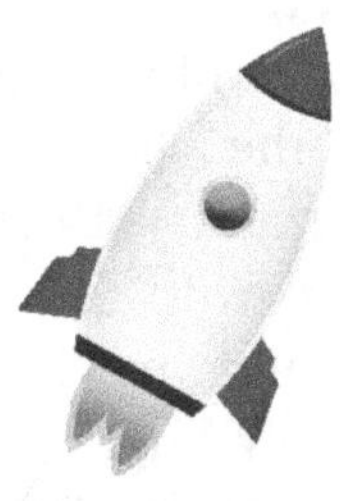

Thursday followed the same pattern as Wednesday. Exercise. Shower. Eat. Cross-stitch. Dinner. Dance. Book.

She forced herself through it to establish various routines. None of them brought her joy, none of them helped the clock jump forward more than forty minutes at a time. But she refused to let the emptiness of the training capsule get to her.

I can do this. This mission to Mars is mine.

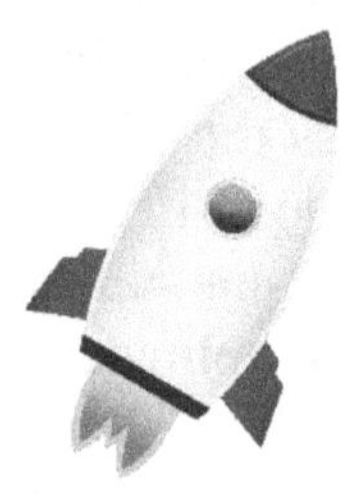

Jenji had planned to go at least a week before utilizing an isolation aid other than routines, but she gave in on day five. She named the microwave Alfred and encouraged it to do a good job boiling her mug of instant coffee.

Humans anthropomorphized things all the time and NASA encouraged the habit as a socialization substitute. Audio interfaces with various pitches, robots with faces, experiments with nicknames, crew habits of thanking machines and patting computers. Heck, everything they flew had names. *Endeavor. Independence. Freedom. Eisenhower. Sagittarius.*

NASA ran a study in 2010 requesting astronauts to write journals for later analysis by NASA staff. They dove into the emotions, triggers, and attention focuses of the astronaut, but the real insight had nothing to do with the journals' words. It turned out the act of daily journaling helped astronauts deal with isolation. Keeping mission notebooks became standard procedure, but Jenji held off on writing one. Going as long as possible without using aids could only prove her mettle.

She might have broken on day five with naming things, but she held out till day seven to use an app on her tablet to write. Only, instead of a daily journal, she wrote letters to Casper.

Jenji would never send them, she had no access to the Internet, but the act soothed her. Plus, she was being a good astronaut using NASA procedures to deal with isolation.

She incorporated letters into her lunch routine, writing while the food cooked, and finishing the letters while she ate.

Day 7
Casper, It's Tuesday again. My second without you. If you were here, I'd tell you how sick I am of this cramped kitchen. How much I miss your voice. Any voice. How, for the first time, I feel... terrified about this mission. I've never had so many nightmares.

Day 10
Casper, I don't think I've ever worked on a cross-stitch so religiously. It might be finished before I leave this place. I squint so much looking at it, I think I need to get reading glasses. Now I feel old.

Day 12
Casper, Today I finally opened the can of mangos, just for something sweet. I ate straight from the can to save water and doing dishes. I can't wait to taste your

cooking again. I want the juiciest burger you can make.

Day 15
Casper, I don't understand this nightmare. I wish I had talked to you about it before this. It haunts my dreams and slips into the day sometimes. And I can't turn around and see you with your silly bumblebee eye mask, can't feel your chest move under my hand. There's no one here to reassure me but me, and I'm awful at it. At least I've gotten used to the cramped kitchen.

Day 17
Casper, I miss you dearly, love. I will bring recordings of your voice with me on this mission to Mars. I want to fall asleep to your singing, wake to your voice encouraging me to get up. Alarm, lullaby, and busy work soundtrack, I want it all to be your voice.

Day 20
Casper, No one can actually take a breath of fresh, Martian air, but I keep imagining what it might be like. Dusty, like an old bookshop? Earthy, like the top of a mountain? I'll touch the red soil, smell the samples, but I'll only be able to guess at the scents outside of a suit. Either way, I'm sure the sight will be beautiful.

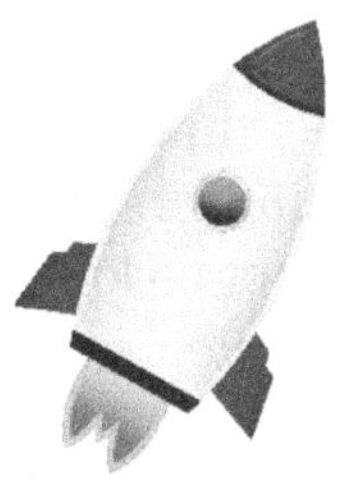

Day twenty-four, she blinked awake and made no move to unzip her sleeping bag.

Jenji felt exhausted and wondered what she looked like on camera. Bags under her eyes? Red eyes? Frail? She'd dreamt of starving to death in the capsule twice the previous night. Stranded in space, not able to look out, staring blankly at a wall while she waited to die.

She went over the dream repeatedly, trying to understand why she kept having it. It proved difficult to choose what soured her mood more, the isolation of the training simulation or fear of the mission going astray. Why was she scared about *this* mission?

Jenji asked herself the question every time she experienced the nightmare but had no answer. She was determined to get one this morning because right now, the allure of her routine wasn't there. The desire to be a lump was too strong. She wanted sleep, and she couldn't get it.

Why, self? What makes this different? All my previous missions had the same dangers. The same chance to mess up. Wrong vectors. Ineffective food or fuel planning. Not completing an objective. Long time away from home. Though this is longer. That it?

Her own mind didn't respond. Jenji sighed. She didn't think the longer time difference had that much of an effect on her mindset, other than perhaps more guilt at leaving Casper for so long.

And of course, being alone.

Alone, alone, alone.

Jenji gazed up at the underside of the bunk above her, her morning brain halfway between the most recent rendition of her nightmare and the logical processing power of an awake mind. It allowed her to make the connection.

Not *being* alone. *Dying* alone.

She died in the nightmares. Cut off from everything outside the ship. No comfort in the sound of human voices or the beautiful sight of stars. No Casper to hold her hand. No crewmate to guide the shuttle back home or help make corrections. No chance of having her ashes spread over the same place as Casper's. Alone in the process of dying and alone after death too.

Jenji closed her eyes. Brought up her memories of looking out into space. Recalled the swelling in her chest as an overwhelming sense of awe filled her. The beauty of space had captivated her in high school, and after being among stars she always heard their siren call in the back of her mind. There was nothing scary about space, for all its vastness and emptiness. It felt as homey as her apartment, but not as warm. Nor as good-smelling, such as when she returned home to see Casper pulling muffins out of the oven or reading while surrounded by various scented candles.

She brought up memories of Casper, how they laughed, how they looked. Turned this moment in real life to a bunch of linked memories. The coolness of the sleeping bag reminded her of her own from when they'd gone camping three years ago in Colorado. The hum of machinery in the walls turned into the washers in the laundromat where they'd met. The stale air the feeling of their bedroom after not leaving it for a full twenty-four hours.

Jenji chastised herself for not bringing a photo of her spouse. Six weeks had felt too short to bother with it, but she missed Casper as much now as she had on her longest time away. The intensity never changed. She imagined their baritone voice reading aloud furniture instructions. A trail of touches on the back of her hand before Casper tangled their fingers with hers as they walked the street. The sight of them, brushing their teeth in the cramped bathroom. Stealing their pillow after they left the bed, enabling Jenji to breathe in the smell of citronella and aftershave. Or raspberry if Casper had felt feminine the previous day.

Pushing herself out of the sleeping bag, Jenji dropped to the floor to start her sit-ups. She'd increased all her reps by ten yesterday. With each touch of her elbows to knees, she added an item to a list called *Ways Casper is With Me*. She'd type them up later.

The memory of their laugh.
The warmth of their hug when they dropped me off.
The memory of their hands braiding my hair.
Their shirt I sleep in.
The ring on my finger.
Their voice in my ear, telling me I got this. I'll be the one chosen for the mission.

She turned over and began her push-ups, imagining that each time her chest got closer to the floor it was getting closer to Casper. Imagined a red string of fate, or a golden linked chain, or a whispered thread of memories going from her heart to theirs. It was invisible. Strong. Endless. It stretched from this isolation chamber to their apartment. It would stretch from Mars to Earth.

When Jenji switched to planks, she counted in togethers. *One together. Two together. Three together.*

There was also an entire team of NASA engineers to make sure she made it back home. Support staff like Nico, who might be watching and counting her tricep dips with her right this very second.

NASA tested everything for peak performance. She had to prove she was front line material, but she would be one part of as perfect a team as NASA could construct. Her team on the ground would be the on the A-list too. All her training for the mission would be hell, to prepare her for the absolute worst, so the actual mission would be a breeze. They wouldn't let anything happen to her, and if something did they'd know how to fix it. Not a single one of her missions had experienced issues. The Mars one wouldn't either.

She clutched her wedding ring tighter. Jenji might not be able to touch Casper, but she knew she had their love and support. Just as the team on the other side of the wall cared for more than her ability to deal with isolation, they wanted to make sure she hadn't starved. Or gone crazy. Or set something on fire in the microwave.

On the mission, she'd talk to photos of Casper. Send daily emails. Follow the tasks NASA sent her. Send and receive audio messages. Greet the Mars colonists. Carry the phantom sense of Casper's arms around her and the well wishes of her team. She might drift in space, the sole occupant of a spaceship, but she wouldn't be alone at all.

Together, together, together, her heart beat.

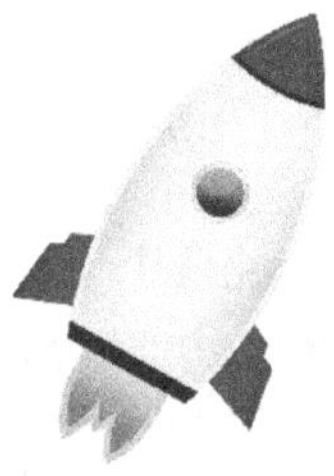

When the doors to the simulation capsule opened, it honestly surprised Jenji. The days had bled into each other, distinguished only by a rotation of meals as she'd finished the cross-stitch days ago.

Nico stepped into the capsule with one of the staff doctors.

"How are you feeling, Stevenson?" Nico asked. "Ready to get out?" He gave her a smile.

Jenji looked around the small, cramped box she'd spent the six weeks in. She'd gotten used to it as she got used to a lot of other things in her life, but yes, she wanted space to run. She wanted to feel the sun on her skin, to kiss Casper silly.

"Yeah, I could leave," Jenji answered, sliding out of the booth where she'd been reading. "Give me five minutes to pack."

"You seem peaceful," the doctor said as Jenji shouldered her pack. "Most candidates are very excited at basic levels of human interaction after six weeks alone."

"I might have been the only one in this room, but I wasn't alone. Not really." She pointed up at one of the cameras in the room and smiled at Nico.

No conversation. No human faces. No one to touch. The six weeks had been long, but so too would be the mission. And being physically isolated didn't mean you were alone. The world's best team stood at her back and the world's best partner lived in her heart.

"The mission to Mars will be easy." Jenji gave a confident shrug.

The doctor smiled back. "I can see that. Now if you follow me, we have some standard tests to conduct."

Jenji fell into step behind her.

ARE YOU REALLY GOING TO COOK THAT?

by J.L. Henker

The aroma of sizzling fat floated out from the ship's galley into the tiny dining hall. Zal frowned. "I don't get it—makes it so dry and tough. What's the point?" he grumped.

Tia licked blood off her claws and shrugged, tearing at the remaining strands left on a bone with her sharp teeth.

Zal leaned sideways in his chair so he could see into the food prep area. "Why's she wearing a sub-hoodie? Looks like she's on an expedition to the ice fields of Dar."

Tia grabbed his arm and pulled him upright. "Stop. That's rude. Humans don't have fur. She's probably cold."

He narrowed his eyes. "You've seen one up close and personal?"

"Very close." Tia grinned.

Zal sucked air between his teeth. "Tia, you didn't! When?"

"Remember the night at Galaxy's End? Tall, red-headed female with tattoos?"

"Not really. I was pretty drunk." He grimaced. "I can't believe you..."

Tia shook her finger at him. "Don't give me attitude, Mr. Left-the-Bar-with-Telusian-Twins."

"But mine had fur," Zal protested.

"Mine did too. Just not all over."

He put his hands on his ears and groaned.

She pinched his arm. "Coward. They're pretty compatible, actually. Two legs, two arms, ears, and..." she tapped his nose, "one of these, just like us."

He batted her hand away. "Stop."

Tia chuckled.

"Why'd the captain decide to hire her?"

Tia burped and set the stripped bone back on her plate. "He needs to find a deposit of ruthenium or he won't be able to afford the upgrade on the fusion reactor. We're running on half-power as it is. She's probably the only geologist he could find on short notice."

"Crap. If she's no good, we won't get paid."

"And the ship ends up on the scrap heap, so be nice and don't give her any trouble."

Loryn marched in from the galley, her hood still pulled tight around her ears, balancing a plate and large mug. She pulled a chair out with her foot and set the items down. She settled across from Zal and rubbed her hands together. "Brr. You keep your ship pretty cold."

Zal frowned. "The captain turned *up* the temperature when you got on board. Now it's too hot."

Tia shook her head. "Ignore him. He'll survive. How's your first week?"

"Good, so far," Loryn said. "The planet has some interesting rock structures."

"It's too dry and warm for me, but we mostly stay on board," Tia said.

"I'd much rather be working on a warm planet than an icy one," Loryn said, hacking at her meat. "Have you been to Dulvaga before?"

"Yep. No luck finding ruthenium," Zal interrupted. "That's where you come in."

Loryn grinned. "Hope I don't disappoint."

"Me too. It sucks not getting paid."

She dropped her knife. "What?"

"Don't pay any attention to him," Tia said, wiping her hands. "The captain always pays us. He was late. Once."

"He hired a scab of a geologist because he's cheap," Zal said. "We came back empty-handed."

Loryn scowled. "I'm not an amateur *and* the captain offered me a fair price. I took this assignment on your *little ship* because I'm young and need more experience, *not* because I'm incompetent."

Tia squinted at Zal. "Nice job tech-boy."

He stopped chewing mid-bite. "I didn't—I mean—you seem—"

"Might want to shut up," she warned.

"—good," he gulped.

Loryn sighed and pulled her hood back. She used both hands to rake fingers through her long, brown hair. Her piercing green eyes narrowed. "Nice to know you don't think I'm a scab. In case you're interested, there's a promising vein on a ridge about two miles from here. I may even get us a bonus."

"Great," Zal said, shoving his chair back to get up.

"Don't go. I have something else to ask you," Loryn said, standing and disappearing into the galley. She emerged with a large bowl of purple berries and leaned over the table. "What are these? Are they edible?"

Zal shoved his snout into the bowl and chomped a mouthful. "Yeaffft, goodft."

Loryn pulled the bowl back quickly, scattering fruit on the floor. "Hey, just wait. If you quit insulting me, I'll make my grandmother's berry pie. It was my ex-girlfriends favorite. I'm good at more things than just rocks."

Zal scrunched his eyebrows. "What's a pie?"

Loryn grinned. "It's a bunch of fruit mixed with spices and sugar. Then you put it into a crust made of flour and butter and bake it."

Zal's face dropped. "You're going to cook them?"

"You'll love it!" Loryn said, pivoting around and scooting back into the galley.

"Hmm," Tia said once Loryn had gone. "She said she had an ex-girlfriend, right?"

"Yeah. so."

"She's cute. I bet she really knows how to cook," Tia said, smiling suggestively.

Zal put his hands over his ears and groaned again.

Tia put her soldering iron on the floor and crawled out from under the control panel. "Hey Zal, I overheard something."

"What? Is the captain going to finally get us the parts to fix the broken cargo lift?"

"No. It's not about the ship. Loryn told the captain she needs access to the interstellar com system in a couple of days to talk with her family."

"Why? Somebody die?"

"No. It's her birthday."

Zal fidgeted. "Yeah. So?"

"We should do something," she said, clenching her jaw. "How do they celebrate?"

Zal stared at her like she had turned into a hissing rockpod snake. "How would I know?"

"Didn't you go through training with some at the Academy?"

"Yeah, but we didn't hang out. They harassed us, called us dog-boys," Zal said, frowning.

"I'm sorry, Zal. I'm surprised you didn't throw them out an air-lock."

Zal grinned. "Nothing so permanent."

Tia pulled out her tablet. "Never mind. I'll just look it up," she said tapping and scrolling down the screen. "Looks like they wear funny hats, eat lots of sticky, gooey stuff and give the person presents."

Zal's eyes narrowed. "You're kidding, right?"

"Take a look." She shoved the screen under his nose.

He peered closely at the tiny video and read the description. "It says here it's a birthday cake.

Tia leaned in. "Why are they lighting it on fire and singing?"

"Dunno. Humans are weird."

Tia poked at the screen. "We need to do that!"

"Seriously, Tia? I don't think so."

She pouted and looked back at the screen. "There's a bunch of supplies in the galley that she used for the pie."

"Trying to impress her?" Zal teased. He yelped as Tia's fist met his shoulder. "That's a yes, I guess. Alright, I'll help." He looked at the screen again. "Have you ever made anything like this before?"

"Nope. But quasars, Zal! If we can figure out how to keep this ancient bucket flying, we can make a cake!"

Zal threw up his hands. "Fine. You read how to make it and give me a list. I'll snoop through her supplies to see if we have what we need. You owe me."

"I've been waiting for you," Tia said, wiping flour off her face with the back of her hand. "Did you find something to make it in?"

Zal slung a clanking bag onto the counter and pulled out two square metal containers. "Will this work?"

Tia studied them approvingly. "Where did you find those?"

He puffed out his chest. "I made them."

"Nice soldering," she said, sizing up the seams. "We have everything we need, except milk. Got some powdered stuff. She even brought fresh eggs."

Zal's eyes brightened. "Lizard?"

"No. Chicken."

He grimaced.

"I found instructions," she said, pointing at a vid screen. She measured and poured ingredients into a bowl and stopped to check the instructions. "It looks pretty simple. Dry ingredients, then wet. Stir. Bake. I'm ready for the eggs. Go ahead."

"How many?"

"Two."

He picked them up and smashed them in his palm, dropping the mess into the mix.

"Not the shells, just the wet part," she yelped.

"Crap." He grabbed a fork and started picking out the shattered pieces.

Tia peered into the bowl. "That's probably good. Stir."

Zal whipped furiously and scooped up a spoonful. It clopped back into the bowl in blobs. "Is it supposed to be lumpy?"

Tia rewound the vid to check. "No, it's too thick. I must have missed something."

Zal checked the instructions. "Did you put in oil yet?"

"That's it!" She poured some into a mug and dumped it in. She snatched the spoon from Zal and beat it some more. "What do you think?"

Zal stuck a finger in and licked his claw. "Doesn't taste bad."

"What now?" Tia asked.

"Cook at three hundred fifty degrees for thirty minutes," he said, his face dropping, "in an oven."

Tia shook the spoon at him. "There's got to be a homesick human on a ship somewhere in the galaxy baking cakes. See if you can find out how to cook it in a thermal induction module."

Zal tapped several times on his tablet and nodded. "Got it."

Tia smeared some oil onto the bottom of the pans and poured in the batter. Zal carefully placed them in the TIM and set the controls.

They stood staring at the glass door for a few minutes. Zal crossed his arms and began to tap his foot. He leaned in closer. "It doesn't look like anything's happening."

Tia pushed him away. "Get out of here and go wipe down the tables or something. You're making me nervous."

He huffed and stomped out. She cleaned up the mess and put everything back in Loryn's storage cabinet. When she finished wiping down the counter, she squinted through the TIM window. The cake had puffed up to the top of the makeshift pans. *Maybe this is going to work.*

Zal poked his head back in the door. "Well?"

"Five more minutes."

He nodded and went back to fidgeting with furniture.

"Hey Zal," Tia yelled as the timer went off, "Get in here. I think they're done."

He charged in and stopped in front of the TIM. Tia opened the door and fragrant warmth rolled into the room.

"How do we know if it's ready?" she asked.

He looked at the recipe. "Poke it with a knife."

Tia pulled a knife from her belt and stabbed it into the middle of the cake

Zal grimaced. "It's not an ice-born bear. You're supposed to poke it, not kill it."

She pulled the knife out and inspected it.

Zal leaned in. "Does it have anything sticky on it?"

"Nope."

"It's done."

Tia yanked the pans out and set them on the counter. They examined their work.

"Is that how it's supposed to look?" Zal asked.

"I don't know. What did the lady in the vid say?"

He scrunched his upper lip. "They should be *nicely browned.*"

They looked down and nodded.

"What's next?" Tia asked.

"It cools down for 10 minutes, then we put that white stuff on top."

When the timer went off, Tia cautiously turned a pan upside-down and let the cake fall out onto a plate.

"That can't be right." She grimaced.

Zal grabbed the pan. "Crap. Half of it's still stuck in there."

Tia snatched it back. "I'll scrape it out and stick it back on. We can use the sticky stuff to cover it up." She scooped out the stuck part, letting it flop back into the gaping hole. She removed the second cake from its pan and pushed a bowl full of frosting in front of Zal. "Do you want to put it on?"

"No!"

Tia poured the white, sugary semi-liquid over the patched cake piece and placed the other half on top. It slid sideways. She pushed it back up and it scooched over the other way. "Zal, get me something to secure this."

He rummaged through a utility drawer and came up with some long sheet metal screws. "Here."

Tia poked them in four different places and finished frosting the cake. It ran down the sides and puddled on the plate. She stood back to admire their work. "We did it!"

Zal pulled up the cake image on his tablet. It wasn't even close. He clicked the screen off before Tia could make a comparison. "Perfect!" he said, grinning.

That evening, Loryn arrived to a full dining hall. If she was surprised the whole crew had shown up at the same time, she didn't let on. They distracted her by asking about the promising vein she'd discovered and how much longer she needed to complete her survey.

When everyone finished eating, Tia and Zal jumped up. They scurried into the galley and returned with the cake, a white emergency candle Zal had salvaged from an old survival kit sparkling proudly on top. They set it down in front of Loryn.

"Happy birthday," they said in unison.

She clasped her hands together and grinned. "How did—I mean, who—oh my gosh, it's wonderful!"

"Don't get too excited," Tia laughed. "You haven't tasted it yet."

Loryn closed her eyes and sat silently for a few moments.

"What's she doing?" Tia whispered in Zal's ear.

"Didn't you pay attention to the video? She's making a wish."

"Oh."

Loryn opened her eyes, leaned forward and blew out the sputtering flame. Everyone clapped and hooted their approval.

"What'd you wish for?" Tia asked.

"I can't tell you."

"Why not?"

"If I do, my wish won't come true." Loryn winked intimately at Tia and took a bite.

Tia smiled and winked back. "Somehow, I think it might."

BULL BY THE HORNS

by E.D. Jones

Content Warning: Bigotry

Let's just dance...this is our last chance...

The cheesy lyrics and retro electronic beat moved through the dancing crowd like enforced nostalgia, which, of course, was what this evening was all about.

"Twenty years," said Sam, looking at Jack, noting the silver streaks in Jack's hair, his face illuminated by the dancing colors of the bar's bioluminescent surface.

"Yeah, I have to drink anytime someone says that," Jack answered, a twang of Texas drawl in his voice. Sam was glad to hear it. Jack had tried to suppress that drawl in college – an adorable affectation, as transparent as it was ineffective – so Sam was glad to hear Jack's real accent unleashed. It didn't hurt that the drawl made Jack somehow even more attractive.

Jack swallowed the last of his martini and slammed the glass down onto the bar.

"You remember that time we went to that country bar and you wrecked your nuts on the saddle of the mechanical bull?" Jack asked.

"Yeah. That sucked," Sam answered.

"The rest of the night didn't. At least…" Jack trailed off.

The two of them turned and leaned against the bar, looking at the people who used to be their classmates, unsure of what to say next. The silence between them was companionable but awkward, the silence of two people who used to be friends – more than that – and were trying to decide how to reconnect.

Jack turned back to the bar and ordered another martini. Sam studiously avoided looking at the synthetic bartender, with its plastic skin and black eyes, that dangerous caricature of humanity. He hadn't ordered a drink yet, because he couldn't bring himself to ask the damn thing for one.

The synth placed a fresh martini in front of Jack.

"And for you sir?" the bartender asked, that digital voice sending ice down Sam's back.

"Nothing," Sam said, teeth gritted. He turned quickly away from the bartender, pushing the anger down. This wasn't the time.

"Let's go talk somewhere more quiet," said Jack.

"Ok, I have to drink anytime someone says that," said Sam, refocusing his attention on Jack. He grabbed Jack's drink and sipped it, then handed it back. Their hands touched, and Sam remembered. And wanted to go back. Twenty years might have passed, but those halcyon college days were still fresh in Sam's memory. And Jack had been a big part of that.

Sam remembered, and regretted.

It hadn't been one thing that had disconnected them. Just...time.

Sam followed Jack into the Hilton's lobby. A holodisplay noted that it was currently 65 degrees and cloudy. They approached the exit, where two synth bellmen held the doors open.

"Have a good night," said one of the synths. Sam lowered his head and pushed past the things as quickly as he could without making a scene.

"I wonder if that bar is still open," said Jack once they were outside.

"The one with the bull? You can't be serious."

"Oh, but I am, *mon ami*. I would love nothing more than to relive that night." Jack grinned a grin that meant trouble. Sam melted into it.

Jack pulled out his com, flicking open a search page.

"Found it," said Jack. "It's like two blocks from here. How crazy is that?"

"Ok, but you get on the bull first," said Sam.

"Nuh-uh," said Jack. "We're recreating that night. That whole night."

"That *whole* night, eh?" Sam knew what Jack was asking, and his answer was a definitive yes.

Jack grabbed Sam's shirt collar and pulled him into a kiss. Sam met it, heat rising within him.

The bar had a synth bouncer. Sam and Jack held up their wrists, and the bouncer scanned their ID chips. A sneer crawled up Sam's lip. The bartender's black eyes registered no reaction that Sam could decipher. *Can't even tell what the damned things are thinking.*

"What's wrong?" asked Jack as the two of them walked into the bar. Old style country music blared, and the crowd wore blue jeans and boots. The mechanical bull stood in the center, unused at the moment. "Besides being a raging synthphobe."

Sam blinked at this. "What?"

"You can't look any of them in the eye," said Jack.

"Yeah, I can." How had *this* become the conversation?

Steeling his nerves, Sam looked one of the synths in its dead little eyes. "See?"

"Well done. Here's your Emmy."

"Hey," said Sam, but he didn't know how to follow that up.

"Look, it's ok, never mind," said Jack. "It's just...you know, back in the day, you and me would have been the ones getting the hate."

Sam stopped in his tracks and stared at Jack, who had started to head to the bar.

"You coming?" asked Jack, looking back over his shoulder.

Part of Sam wanted to just turn around and walk out. Here was Jack, a guy Sam hadn't seen in a lot of years, a guy who had once been the center of Sam's world, but who was now a stranger with twenty years of history that Sam didn't know. And Jack had the gall to just walk back into Sam's head and start trying to renovate it?

"Hey, I'm sorry, I didn't mean to—"

"You did though," said Sam. He turned to leave. "See you in another twenty years maybe."

"Sam," he heard Jack say. Sam stopped. He felt Jack's hand on his shoulder. He turned around to face Jack. Those eyes, those big, stupid, blue eyes, those eyes he'd fallen into a thousand times in college. Sam fell into them again. He breathed deep and shrugged it off as best he could, even as Jack's words, Jack's judgment, began turning wheels.

"Ok," he said. "Drop the synth shit."

Jack nodded. "Done. You go get your ass on that bull, and I'll get us drinks."

Sam approached the bull and scanned his chip to pay the fee. He set the difficulty level to 1, climbed into the saddle, and pressed start. He could see Jack grinning at him as the crowd gathered to watch this city slicker get humiliated.

The movement started easy enough, and Sam felt like he was holding his own, but after a few seconds Sam slipped forward in the saddle, flailed, and fell, landing face-down on the vomit-smelling mat. The crowd cheered. He stood, gave a bow, and walked back to Jack, who handed him a drink. Sam downed it in one gulp.

"Ok, now I've done *that*, can we please do something more fun?"

"Mais bien sur," said Jack. He opened his com and ordered a taxi. The two of them left the bar.

Sam couldn't get the synth thing out of his head. He felt Jack judging him, and he hated it.

"I just don't trust synths, ok?" Sam said. "Not since..."

But he couldn't get the words out. He looked down.

"What happened?"

Jack's concern hit Sam hard. Everything boiled over, the rage, the loss, the memory of it all.

The fire.

Sam lost control, and tears flowed. He felt Jack wrap those big hairy arms around him.

"You don't have to—"

Sam looked up and met Jack's eyes, and the whole story tumbled out.

"There was an accident. Or so the company claimed after the fact. I'm not so sure. My boyfriend at the time had an early model synth as a housekeeper. There was a fire. It looked like an accident, and maybe it was, maybe it was just that the synth was faulty, like those early self-driving cars. But the damn thing left the stove on. It left the stove on. How stupid is that? Something so simple. Such an easy, stupid mistake. And...I lost everything."

The last part was hardest to say, but he got the words out, quietly, trembling.

"Including him."

Jack drew in a sharp breath. "I'm—" he started.

"So that's the story," Sam said, steadying his breathing. Somehow, telling Jack felt right, felt like a kind of catharsis, and the pain of it felt a little less sharp. Still there, still raw, but a piece of the pain had changed shape.

The taxi arrived. "Western boarding house, on Flint," said Jack. The synthetic driver nodded, and the taxi slid into the electric night.

The synth looked at Sam in the rearview. Sam looked away. He knew, rationally, that he shouldn't hate all of them. Jack was right, damn him, and now some of Sam's revulsion felt a little bit wrong.

He didn't *hate* them, really. Did he?

What was the difference between hate and fear?

Jack said nothing to Sam during the cab ride, but he grabbed for Sam's hand, and Sam let him hold it.

Jack's "boarding house" was actually a twee little boutique hotel in an Old West theme. *Of course he's staying here.* Jack had always pretended his love of all things "country" was ironic and meta, but Sam knew better. The guy had been a closet cowboy as long as Sam had known him. Of all the things to feel self-conscious about, Jack had always been a little bit embarrassed to be a little bit country. And Sam had always found that to be a little bit adorable.

The two of them got out of the cab. The empty sidewalk shone with recent rain, and the air smelled of petrichor.

"I'm sorry," Jack said, struggling to meet Sam's eyes.

"It's ok," Sam said. "Somehow, I think I needed that."

There was a café open next door to the boarding house, and the two of them headed inside. Sam felt warm light and good music wrap around him like a blanket, and he started to feel a little better.

The barista was human, so Sam was thankful for small mercies. He ordered a decaf latte, and Jack ordered a chai. They sat together at a table in the back.

"I have a story about synths too," said Jack. "It's nothing compared to what you went through, but..."

"Tell me," said Sam.

"I lost a good job to a synth. At the time, it felt like I was losing a career."

"What happened?"

"I was working as a data analyst at a big company downtown – you might have heard of it – Voight?"

"Yeah," said Sam. "They were working on AI gaming stuff, right?"

"AI, VR, AR, the whole bit. Anyway, the company brought in some synths as temps to do data entry."

"They can do that?"

"To a point, and that point was apparently profitable for the company."

"But surely they couldn't do your job, right?"

Their drinks arrived, and Sam thanked the barista. He took a sip of his latte. It warmed him.

"That's what I thought," said Jack. "I was wrong. Actually, I was right – they certainly couldn't do my job as well as I could – but again, profits. At the time, synths were free labor."

"Ah, so it was that long ago," said Sam.

"Yeah, before the law changed."

"Damn," said Sam. "I'm sorry."

"Anyway, I don't want to bore you with all that," said Jack. "I lost my job and had a hell of a time finding another."

"So we've both been fucked over by synths," said Sam.

"We've both been fucked over by circumstances outside of our control," said Jack.

Sam thought about this. The two drank their coffees in silence for a few moments.

"I could hate synths because they stole my job," said Jack. "But instead, you know what I hate?"

"What?"

"Nothing."

"Really," said Sam, halfway between a question and incredulity.

"Hate is damage," Jack continued. "Hate lets the bad guys win."

Hate lets the bad guys win. Sam chewed on this for a bit.

"You're saying I need to disconnect the trauma of the fire from the synth who started it."

"Basically," said Jack. "And that will be hard as hell. It's going to take time. And you need to talk to a professional about it."

"That much I know," Sam said. He'd had a therapist for a little while, but he kept forgetting to schedule another session, and then, well, time happened. He made a mental note to call on Monday.

"That's the thing about trauma," said Jack. "It lies to us. It gives us targets and tells us we should blame them, even if those targets are completely irrational."

Sam finished his latte. "Look, I'm sorry. I didn't want this whole evening to turn into a 'fix Sam's damage' thing."

"It hasn't," said Jack, putting his hand on top of Sam's hand on the table. "Honestly."

Sam kissed Jack, surprising himself with how quickly it felt natural to do so. He breathed in Jack's scent and remembered.

Jack broke off the kiss and gave Sam a smirk. "Now that's more like it," he said. "Come on then." Jack stood and headed for the exit. Sam followed, a little dazed.

Trauma lies to us. Hate lets the bad guys win. They seemed like such simple statements, but they swirled around Sam's mind as he followed Jack up the stairs of the boarding house.

A synth was walking down the hallway toward them. Sam pushed down the fear and revulsion he felt looking at that inhuman face, the skin the color of a corpse, the lidless black eyes, the mechanical way the thing walked. He took a deep breath, met the synth's eyes, and gave it a nod in greeting. He saw Jack see him make this effort, as minimal as it was, and smile.

I'll work on it, Sam resolved. *I promise.*

Jack entered his room and turned on the light, and Sam followed, closing the door behind him. He looked at Jack, and every thought but one melted away.

Jack slammed Sam against the door, kissing him senseless. Sam gave into it, wrapping himself around Jack, taking him to the bed. Memories flooded back of a college life long gone and half-forgotten. The two of them staying up all night talking philosophy, young minds trying to figure out who they were.

And the two of them not talking. The night that Sam had ridden the bull, the two of them had finally gotten past the bullshit and found each other.

SCION

by Summer Jewel Keown

Alys counted the children as they wriggled in the exitroom. Seven, eight...where was nine?

"Elin!" she called out, her voice echoing, lending a bit more sternness to its tone than she really meant to. A giggle from behind the rack of breathing apparatuses gave their hiding place away. "Ok, my silly young friend. Come on out." The child emerged from behind the gear, mildly chastened, their enthusiasm palpable. Alys patted them on the head and directed them back to the group.

"Now everyone, listen up. I know you're all very excited for our field trip, but before we go, please repeat the rules back to me. Ok?"

The children nodded, their eyes wide and shining.

"Tell me, when we go outside, what do we wear?"

"Leis!" they responded in unison. Alys suppressed a smile.

"What do the leis do?"

"Help us breathe!"

"And do we ever take them off?" This was the most important question. Alys leaned forward to gauge the children's expression.

"No!" They seemed as sincere as she could expect.

"Even if they're itchy?"

"Not even if they're itchy!"

"Well done." Alys clapped her hands at their enthusiasm. "Will everyone please form a line so that we can get suited up?"

In truth, Alys was as excited as the children. Alys had always loved Outdoor Day. This was the fourth year in a row she got to take her class out and it never got old. Seeing their faces when they stepped out was almost as good as the experience itself.

Each child came up to her in turn and waited as patiently as an eight-year-old could wait to receive one of the apparatuses from the wall, to have Mx. Alys place it carefully around their necks. Each cord of lightweight mesh, wrapped with nylex vines, woke up as she ran a finger gingerly across it. It was as though it also was looking forward to the trip outside.

Once all of the children were properly equipped, Alys took one for herself and slid it over her head. The nylex vine pulsed against her skin as it adapted to the cadence of her breath.

"Ready?" Alys asked, giving the group one last look-over.

A chorus of "yes!" rang out and Alys turned to tap in the sequence that would unlock the door. It wasn't as though the code was a secret - it was written on a tab kept just on top of the computer - but they didn't want any of the youngsters to accidentally wander out without proper protection.

There was a hiss as the door slid open and the oxygen from their containment room escaped. Alys waved the children through and followed behind, pulling the door shut behind her and listening to be sure that the latch clicked.

As she turned, the brightness of the suns blurred her vision and Alys squinted her eyes nearly closed. She let the warmth cover her. As she had on each of her trips before, she felt something in her open, something she couldn't feel in their carefully enclosed, purified and pressurized community pod.

Before she even opened her eyes, she could feel her vine begin to work. Its nylex leaves stretched out and began to help her breathe, converting the gasses in the air into oxygen and wafting it up toward her nose and mouth. Amazing, really. It had only been in the last five years that they had been able to do this. To go outside without a full protective suit. For regular folk to leave the pod and see more of this new world of theirs. She thanked the gods and their science for making this possible.

Opening her eyes, Alys couldn't help but grin. She tried to imagine what it was like for the kids, experiencing all of this for the very first time. The suns above them in their pink and turquoise-swirled sky. The spiny plants growing tall from the rocky surface, bursting into clusters of green leaves several feet above their heads, a few topped with gloriously huge purple and orange striped flowers. There was something that simply could not be matched about the incredible openness of it all, and about this growing plant life reaching up so high against gravity.

What would it have been like if she could have been outdoors as a child? But back then, there hadn't even been an outdoors to escape to. Just the blackness that surrounded them as they hurtled through it toward hope. As it was, she had only been outside the first year it was possible for someone of her role. She was twenty then. For a few years before that, it was a carefully meted out privilege for the scientists and the builders only. Back when they had to wear cumbersome, protective suits. Before nylex was perfected, making this all possible. That first day she stepped outside, she cried and shook and prayed and smiled until her face hurt.

The kids ran in circles under the open sky, calling to one another. She watched them carefully to ensure their leis stayed on. If one fell off, she would have a minute or two to return it, so it wasn't particularly dangerous, but still, she took all of the precautions.

She gave them a few minutes to enjoy, then gathered them back together.

"Are we ready to take our walk to the Science Center? There are all kinds of very smart people there who know a lot of very neat information, and some of them are going to talk to us today. And who knows, maybe some of you will grow up to live and work there."

The kids nodded in the affirmative. Alys noticed Rhys craning to lick his vine and she coughed to get his attention. He quickly stopped and pretended he was doing nothing of the sort.

"Off we go. Please keep up and follow me!"

Alys led them down the winding path that led toward the Science Center. The path looked like a neutral-toned mosaic and she marveled, not for the first time, that they had built something not just useful but beautiful here. A form rose up in the distance: the large, stately building that was their destination.

"Wooooow," Mari said, her mouth hanging wide open.

"Wow, indeed, Mari," Alys replied.

"Can we really work there someday?"

"If you want to be a researcher, absolutely. You will have to study, and work very hard, but then you can discover wonderful things. Things that will make our lives better. Like these leis that let us breathe outdoors. The air out here is mainly carbon dioxide, which is a gas. We cannot breathe it on our own, but we are lucky, because the leis breathe it for us. They turn it into oxygen. Isn't that wonderful?"

Mari nodded, then ran to catch up to Rhys, who was always the most adventurous of the group, to Alys's joy, and often her chagrin as well. One or more of these children would probably help them make the next advances on this world. Maybe one of them would finally figure out how to let them live outside of the pods. To breathe on their own. To have a window that opened.

She wondered how their lives would be different even five, ten years in the future. Alys liked to think that they had been cooped up so long traveling here that once they had their feet on solid ground that they couldn't help but run. After all, it had been only ten years since they arrived and already...all of this.

As they neared the Science Center, they could see people bustling around within it, clad in the pale pink jumpsuits that indicated their roles as researchers. The children rushed to the door, where a jumpsuit-clad young man waited just behind its tinted doors, smiling.

Alys reached up and touched the screen that would convey her voice inside.

"Alys Onai and my class. We are here for a presentation."

The man waved his hand over a pad, cuing the door to slide open for them. The children shuffled into the entryway, chattering at a nearly unintelligible speed and pointing at the things they could see through the glassy barrier. Once the door slid shut again and they heard it click, the air circulation came on.

Alys helped the kids hang their leis up on a rack to recharge for the trip back. The inside of the Science Center was pressurized similarly to the pod at home, though Alys had heard it was a more updated system and that their oxygen percentage was higher. She made a mental note to ask one of the researchers to explain it to the class.

The interior door slid open and their host smiled and waved them in. He looked to be about Alys's age. She felt a pang of envy. A recollection snuck in of studying biochemistry at age twelve, getting an A on a test and her teacher praising her heavily. Of Mx. Locke sending a message to her father suggesting that she consider the science track. And then her father rolling his eyes when he read it, telling her she wasn't cut out for such a rigorous course of study. But it was fine, Alys thought, shoving the memory back into the dark corner of her mind where it belonged. What she did now was important, and maybe she could help some of these kids along their way.

"Hello," the scientist said. "I'm Dr. Jónsson. I'm a junior researcher here at the Center, and I'll be your guide today. We'll start with a presentation in the auditorium and then I'll give you a look around. How does that sound?"

"That sounds super awesome!" Rhys yelled. The other kids quickly matched his enthusiasm. They followed Dr. Jónsson down a long day-lit hallway, toward the presentation room.

"Look Mx. Alys," Elin said. "Outside the window. That lady isn't wearing a lei! How is she doing that?" The children pointed frantically, practically pasting themselves to the window.

"Ooohhh she's breaking the rules," Rhys shouted. "She's going to be in so much trouble."

Alys walked toward the window, her brow wrinkled. Surely they were mistaken. They must just not be able to see the woman's lei. Perhaps it was a newer model.

She peered out into the sunshine. There was a woman out there, walking and seeming to talk to herself. Alys squinted. At first glance, the children did seem to be correct. She didn't see a lei hanging from the woman's neck. Her hair was pulled back, so it wasn't simply hidden. How odd.

All of them staring at her must have tripped her senses, because just then, the woman turned toward them. Alys could only imagine how this looked, a bundle of children smashed against the window, eyes wide, pointing at her. An amused look crossed the woman's face as she turned. Her eyes scanned over their group and then came to rest on Alys. She waved.

Alys felt rooted to the ground. The woman was lovely. No, lovely was not a strong enough word. Striking, perhaps. Stunning. Extraordinary. Shoulder-length braids were pulled into a twist, then cascaded down her back. And she wore a crown of the brilliant orange and purple flowers they had seen on their walk from the pod. Alys found herself wanting to reach out and touch one, to hold it in her hand and take it home with her so that she could remember this strange, astonishing woman later. But she knew that this vision would not fade, even if she had nothing tangible to hold onto.

Their eyes met, and the woman's gaze held Alys still. Warm brown, flecked gold in the sunlight, they held a softness within them that made her want to rush out and introduce herself. Maybe even to drop down on one knee and propose like they did in the old days.

But that was ridiculous. What was she thinking?

One edge of the woman's lips turned up into a crooked smile. Alys felt as though her heart had dropped down into her feet. She lifted her hand to wave back.

The scientist who had been leading them coughed. Alys jumped at the sound. "Shall we?" the scientist said.

"Yes, of course. Children, please follow Dr. Jónsson. We have so much to learn."

When Alys turned back to the window, the woman was already gone. But where? She felt a tug at her heart, as though she'd experienced a loss. But that was silly, of course. She reluctantly followed the children down the hall.

The children were enraptured by Dr. Jónsson's presentation but Alys heard none of it. She could think of nothing but the woman with the flower crown. Her eyes. That smile. The light on her face. She couldn't recall ever having a reaction like this to anyone before. But she would probably never see her again. After all, she only brought the children here once a year for a few hours.

After a video showing the kids the life of microscopic creatures, Dr. Jónsson answered many of the questions volleyed at him before raising his hands in defeat.

"Ok, everyone," the scientist said. "Those are all great questions. Let's hold any more till the end. Who wants to go see a real life laboratory?"

The kids all cheered in the affirmative. Alys grinned. Seeing their love of learning never got old. They tromped out of the auditorium behind Dr. Jónsson.

"Mx. Alys, can you believe we have little creatures in our eyelashes?" asked Celissa, the youngest of her charges.

Alys would have preferred not to think about that, but Celissa seemed more fascinated than grossed out, so she forced a smile. "Isn't our world fascinating?" she asked.

"How many do you think there are?" Rhys asked, pulling his eyelid out as though he might be able to catch a glimpse. "I want to name them all."

The lab was not far from the presentation room. Dr. Jónsson led them inside. Light shone down from large skylights in the room, which was teeming with plants of all kinds.

"Wow," she said. It looked so different from the last time she had been here. She'd expected it to look more sterile, to feel cold and clinical. They didn't have anything like this in the pod. Sure, there were the carefully tended plants under hot grow lights but these were lush and wild.

"Beautiful aren't they?" The voice from behind her was soft and deep and Alys knew who it was without even turning around. She couldn't explain how she knew, she just did.

"Dr. Witkowski, what a pleasure," Dr. Jónsson said, his voice not quite concealing surprise and perhaps a little awe.

Alys turned to face her. The woman—no, the Doctor—had a hint of a smile on her lips and a sparkle in her eyes. That's why it took Alys a moment to take in the rest.

Green tendrils wrapped around her neck as though they grew from beneath her skin. And that's when Alys realized that the beautiful orange and purple flower she'd noticed behind the Doctor's ear wasn't just decorative. It was part of her. All of this was.

As the Doctor breathed in and out, the vines seemed to pulse in time. Not so different from the leis they used to travel from the pod, but flesh and blood and plant as one. They were strange and wrong, as though some deep, unspoken rule had been broken. Alys felt overcome, almost ill. She couldn't stop staring.

"Hello children," Dr. Witkowski said, unconcerned under Alys's focused gaze. "I consider myself very fortunate to meet you today during your visit. Back when I was your age, I was already very much in love with science—botany and biology, mostly—and I knew that it would be my future. Perhaps some of you may follow a similar path."

"Are you a plant lady?" Elin burst out. "How do you have them all over you like that?"

"Elin," Alys admonished. "It's not polite to ask people questions about their bodies."

The doctor laughed. "It's all right. She's only curious. I know I would be as well. To start with, let's see how much you know. Why is it that we cannot breathe outside?"

"Not enough oxygen," Celissa said quietly, clearly a bit intimidated.

"Exactly. Which is why we have always lived in pods that can make that oxygen for us. We have tried for so many years to change this world to fit us. But one day, as I was walking outside, wearing one of those cumbersome old versions of a lei, an idea came to me that changed my life. And it was this: What if there was a way that we could adapt ourselves to the world outside, instead of changing it to suit us? It was my theory that we could do so. And it seems that perhaps I was correct."

The doctor turned her neck for the children to examine her more closely. Where the vines grew into her skin and underneath, the network of green was visible under her skin.

"Can I touch it?" asked Rhys.

"I would prefer not," she replied. "Are you ticklish?"

"Yes..." Rhys said, nerves apparent.

"It is a little bit like being tickled, and that is not a sensation I enjoy. My vines are very sensitive."

"The flowers," Alys said aloud, immediately clapping a hand over her mouth. She hadn't meant to say it out loud.

The doctor turned her gaze to Alys. "I'm sorry," she said, "I didn't introduce myself properly. I'm Dr. Witkowski, but you can call me Maab."

"I'm...Mx. Alys. Onai. I mean, just Alys. You can call me anything, or Alys is fine." She clamped her mouth shut before she could embarrass herself any further.

"It is wonderful to meet you, Alys. And yes, my flowers." She smiled. "A bit of a flourish, I suppose, but also research. When one uses one's self as a test subject, you can try a few things. I imagine us all able to express ourselves through the plants that become part of us, those who volunteer."

"Volunteer?"

"Indeed. We have many goals here at the Science Center but the central one is this: We believe we can live outside of the pods, in the open air. We simply have to adapt. It looks different, I know. It feels different. Symbiotic. We have tested it, as you can see on myself, and now we are accepting volunteers who also want to take on the graft and help us make this next transition.

Alys wanted to say something back, but she was speechless. Not only was the Doctor beautiful, but she was brilliant. A visionary. So much more intelligent than her.

The kids all shouted out their questions but Dr. Jónsson broke in. "We are just about at the end of our time for the day, students. And Dr. Witkowski has many important things to do."

"Awww ok," Elin complained.

"What do we say, children?" Alys asked, in her best teacher voice.

"Thank you Doctor!" they shouted.

Alys didn't want to leave, but there was no other choice. She locked eyes with the Doctor one last time, then led the children out of the room, out of the Science Center, then all the way back home.

Alys lay in her bunk, her thoughts a whirl around her. Yesterday she knew nothing about Dr. Witkowski—no, Maab—and today she wanted to know nothing but her.

She jerked upright. It was clear. She had to speak with her again, just the two of them.

No. She lay back down, staring up at the ceiling. That was ridiculous. What would she say?

They were taking volunteers to be grafted. But of course that wouldn't apply to her. Surely it was too late to chart a different path now. Or was it?

Could she actually bring herself to do it? To change her body, to risk everything? Would she be doing it for science, or for *her*? And did it matter?

Laying in her bunk, restless, Alys felt the minutes as they slowly passed achingly by. An hour left before time to rise, she knew she would be getting no sleep. But sleep didn't matter now. She knew now what she was going to do.

Alys rose, dressed, and made her way to the exitway. The leis hung quietly in the dim predawn light. Was she really going to do this?

Her heart beat a quick rhythm in her chest. In the exitroom, she hung a lei around her neck. Carefully tracing its leaves with her fingers, Alys tried to imagine what it would be like with vines like these not just on her skin but in it, connected to her like veins. She wished she would have asked Maab what it felt like to stand under the sun and absorb its rays like food, like breath.

She punched the code and took a deep breath as she yanked the door open. It was cool in the predawn air. She'd never been out this early before. The air was suffused with a chilly magic. Perhaps it was anticipation, or maybe fear.

The path seemed longer somehow, walking it alone, but soon she was back at the familiar building. Its lights were dimmed but she could see a few people around inside.

Last chance to turn back, she thought. But she knew what she wanted. She touched the screen. After a moment, a figure appeared through the two sets of doors. With the light behind them, Alys could only see a shadow.

"Yes?" a voice asked through the speaker. "How can we help you?"

She barely got the words out. "I'm here to volunteer. For the grafting."

The door in front of her slid open and she hung her lei with care. If all went well, this might be the last time she ever needed one. As the interior door slid open to permit her entry, Alys looked up into the face she most wanted to see in the world.

"You came back," Maab said, that dazzling smile focused on her, and her alone. "I was so hoping you would."

GETAWAY

by Tucker Struyk

Content Warning: Homophobia

Across the street from an airport parking lot, Noah thumbed through a news app as strong winds rolled over the cornfield behind him. He skimmed headlines until a Buick Park Avenue veered to a halt by the curb. The driver cracked a window and surveyed the area—all three stragglers and Noah himself. "Are you with the dial-a-ride service?" Noah asked.

The driver raised a brow. "Noah Sanders?"

"Yes, sir."

"Hop in."

Noah opened the back door and sat down. Inside, food wrappers lined the car's interior and the stench of cigarette smoke hung stale in the air. The driver extended a hand and Noah shook. "The name's Jim. Jim Barnes."

"Pleased to meet you."

The car bumped down a potholed road until the wheels met a slick gravel surface to sail across for miles. Pebbles popped beneath their weight. The shattered bits clanged against the car's underbelly. For nearly half an hour Jim did not speak, but Noah felt his gaze in the rearview mirror. Yet, each time Noah checked, Jim kept his eyes on the road. Jim broke the quiet and asked, "What brought you to town?"

"Am I that obvious?"

Jim smirked but made no reply.

Noah twiddled with the surgeon cuff on his tweed jacket. He found himself tongue-tied. Growing up closeted, he never knew when to be open about his husband. Especially somewhere only a state over from his hometown. Donn did not have that issue. He found it effortless to be queer in rural settings because he never lived in one. Finally Noah said, "My partner and I bought a summer home in town."

"Ah," said Jim, "too early to vacation here." His tongue clicked in a *tsk* sound as he picked at coffee-stained teeth with the thumbnail of his free hand. "Spring is tornado season. Much better to come back in the summer." He nodded to an empty backseat. "Where's the Mrs. then? Packed in the luggage?" His laughter filled the car.

Noah twirled the gold band around his ring finger. He thought to correct Mrs. to Mr. but decided against it. No need to ruffle feathers. "I came early to check on what needs fixing before our romantic getaway," he said.

"Oh, I see." Jim flicked half chewed jerky to the floormat. "Getting a jump on the housework before you get an earful from the wife. Smart move."

"I suppose you could look at it that way."

"What's the old ball-and-chain doing while you're here?" Jim laughed again. "Better keep an eye on your credit card bill."

"There's some important conference for the biotech firm," said Noah. "It ought to keep the whole department busy for me, so no worries there." He minced his words to avoid a gendered statement.

Jim sat upright and cracked his neck. "Biotech," he spat. "Tell her to be careful." His fingers tapped the steering wheel. "She's getting in bed with snakes. Don't be surprised when they bite."

"What makes you say that?"

Jim let his eyes wander as a barn came into view. The first structure Noah had seen since the paved road. "I used to be a farmer," said Jim. To his left, in a field, a tractor skimmed the flat-lined horizon. Mounted behind the tractor, a seeder tore into topsoil like a knife through tissue paper. "A few rotten seasons put me in a bind and I couldn't afford the seeds anymore." He brought a cola can to his lips. "Biotech." Took a sip. "Goddamn vultures."

Noah turned to the window. His eyes fixed on air bubbles in the tint. "I know what you mean," he said. Jim squinted at him in the mirror. "I was recently laid off at a company I spent nearly a decade at." Noah waved a dismissing hand. "The insurance industry has been in shambles ever since the weather went to shit." A wall cloud gathered outdoors. "It's funny. We spend our whole lives chasing one thing after the next. A job, a degree, a partner, then a better job, and now a baby." The car exhaust rattled and hissed. "We forget nature has the last word. Always."

The old Buick lurched to the right as a soft pocket of gravel gave way underneath, then they gradually straightened out. Jim shook his head. "Ain't that the truth," he muttered. "All anyone can do is protect what's theirs. Or try to anyway."

The two listened to country music on the radio until Jim turned down a long driveway up to a prairie-style house neighbored by a private lake. A rustic home comprised of cedar logs and stone columns to accent the cabin aesthetic. Tucked just behind the tree line, a path was cut along the county road—wide enough to drive an ATV through. Noah stepped out to the scent of cut grass and pine trees. Jim popped the trunk. "Let me help you with your bags."

"Thank you," said Noah, "but there's really no need." He slipped Jim a twenty dollar tip. "This tête-à-tête has been a delight. To ask for more would be taking advantage."

Jim stopped himself on his way to the car. "I should tell you," he said, "I've got a buddy—he's a good guy. A handyman. He might be able to take a load off the housework for you." He handed Noah a crinkled business card. Noah accepted the scrap of paper with gratitude, then slid it in his pocket to forget about later.

Jim took the car out of park. "It's been nice talking to you." He placed the bill in his shirt pocket. "I'm sure we'll see each other around. Not many drivers around here." He took his foot off the brake. "I look forward to meeting your wife."

Noah swung bag straps over his shoulders and lugged his suitcase up a stone staircase, then turned with a polite grin. Jim offered a toothy simper in return. Noah made certain the car drove out of sight as he waved Jim off the property.

It was not until late that afternoon when Jim's tread worn tires traversed the drive to Noah's doorstep. "You weren't kidding about seeing me soon," he said.

Jim chuckled. "That's small town life for you." He peeled off the drive and onto the road without abandon. To him, there was no fear of a fellow driver. The odds were in his favor. "Where are you headed?"

"Uh, nearest grocer, I guess." Noah scratched his head. "Wherever I can get a lightbulb and some food. You'd know better than me."

"I've got you covered."

The car bobbed across the uneven road, headed closer to a dusty highway exit that the nearest town catered to. Noah's phone vibrated in his pocket. A call from Donn. He slid the answer key. "Hey, babe. How's the conference?"

Jim clicked the radio volume down a couple notches. His ears pricked. Noah prayed the male voice on the other end was inaudible. "There's really not much work left to do. I'm picking up a bulb for a flickering light now, but other than that it's in good shape," said Noah. He pressed his palm against the phone speaker to buffer sound. "Well, I miss you. I can't wait for you to arrive tomorrow. The place feels so empty without you." He giggled. "Oh, really? I'm going to hold you to that." A smartphone ad played on the radio. The latest model promised a high quality camera lens. "Alright, I love you too. Bye."

Jim turned the radio back up. Neither spoke for a while. The road came to a plywood paneled island in a dirt parking lot. "We're here," said Jim. "This is the shop." He pulled in as close to the front door as he could get. "I'll wait out here for you."

"Thank you." Noah gave Jim another tip. "I'll be in and out."

He swung open the shop door and nearly bumped into the shopkeeper as she brushed dust off merch on the impulse-buy rack. He weaved around her and into the store. "Pardon me," he said. "That's what I get for not looking where I'm going."

The shopkeeper brushed off her work apron. Her name tag read Mrs. Carter. "I'm the one who should be apologizing." She tossed her duster over the counter. "What can I help you with?"

Noah surveyed the store but saw no aisle markers. "Lightbulbs?"

Mrs. Carter pointed a wrinkled finger. "Third aisle from the far end." She walked in that direction. "Let me show you." Noah followed.

Her doddery footfalls echoed as her wedge heels tapped on the laminate flooring. Half a dozen shelves filled the shop. The middle aisle was for hardware and home repair. Mrs. Carter brought him to their houseware. Noah picked a standard bulb. "This is the one," he said. "Thanks for your help."

"I'll ring you up at the cash register." Mrs. Carter passed fresh corn in rattan produce baskets. "If you like sweet corn, get some while it's in stock."

Noah grabbed a piece with enough husk torn to reveal its bare kernels. He jabbed a thumb into an exposed kernel and felt tough resistance. Nothing like the corn he grew up with. The crop needed time to ripen. "I think I'll stick with the lightbulb," he said. "Thank you though." Mrs. Carter stared at the corncob he held. "Looks a bit green for my taste."

She thrust her head back. "You're 'a bit green' yourself."

Noah furrowed his brow. "I beg your pardon."

She backpedaled to the register. "I didn't mean anything by it." Her birthstone bracelet rattled against a nickel silver bangle band as she scanned his item. "Folks around here just aren't used to tourists this time of year." She slid his credit card a couple times before the machine processed his purchase. "Not during tornado season."

Noah nodded along. His patience waned with the setting sun. He snagged the bag from her loose grip. "Thank you." A bell jingled above the door as he left.

Mrs. Carter waved. "Come again soon."

Standing on the third highest rung on a teetering ladder, Noah unscrewed the flickering lightbulb in the sunroom and placed it on the pail shelf. He screwed in the new bulb, climbed down, and flipped the switch. Still the light flickered. His index finger and thumb rubbed the bridge of his nose. This was more than a worn out bulb.

He found the crumpled card stashed in his back pocket. In between creases he read the name Mason Hayward and began to dial the number. The line rang. "Hello," answered a gruff voice.

"Hi," said Noah. "I've got a faulty wiring issue at my new place here in town. Jim Barnes said you could help."

"The house by Lake Humphrey?" Mason asked.

Noah's head recoiled from the phone. He scratched the back of his neck and brought the speaker back to his ear. "Yeah. How did you know?"

"I did some work for the previous owners." Noah tugged at his shirt's neckline, as he fiddled with the tag. He figured Jim had made Donn and him the talk of the town. A couple of clueless city folk who rolled in with the swelling storm. "I could fit you in tomorrow morning," said Mason.

"Sounds good," said Noah. "See you—" Mason hung up –"then."

Noah saw movement outside the window. A Chevy Tahoe pulled into the driveway with a cloud of dust billowing behind it. The sky took on a greenish hue. The trees laid still in the dying breeze. Noah went outside smiling.

Donn opened the car door in a plaid shirt and denim jacket. Noah rushed to meet him in a warm embrace. Noah held him close enough for their rib cages to press. The smell of lavender wafted from Donn's hair. "When did you get in?" Noah asked. "I thought you weren't coming until tomorrow."

Donn pulled away from their hug to grab his luggage. "The conference ended early, so I thought I'd surprise you." He offloaded the bags onto Noah. "Do you like the rental? It might be overkill, but it was the only car at the lot with a sunroof and I thought we could afford to treat ourselves."

Noah shook his head. "Who cares about the car?" He wrapped an arm around Donn and guided him over the porch steps. "What do you think of this house?"

Donn craned his neck up at the portico as they entered. "It looks great." He traced the grooves in the wood railing on the staircase. His eyes gravitated to the single tier chandelier. "Just like we pictured it."

Noah planted a kiss on Donn's forehead. "Yes, it is."

"My mom makes a pretty good realtor, right?" said Donn. "She missed her calling." He turned to Noah. "You went to the store earlier, right?" He paused. "How're the locals?"

Noah shrugged. His eyelids sank heavy when he blinked. "Oh, you know," he said, "typical Midwest hospitality. Big smiles and casual pleasantries, you know, that kind of stuff." His hands slid inside his pockets and his shoulders tensed. "This place is perfect. You're going to love it."

Donn awoke to knocks at the door. He groaned. "Who could that be?" he asked. "We just got here."

Noah walked to the bedroom window. A work van was parked next to the Tahoe. "Must be the handyman."

"Handyman? I thought you said the place was perfect."

"It is." Noah yawned. "There's just a little faulty wiring. No problem." The doorbell rang thrice. "We'll have it taken care of in no time."

Noah dressed and answered the door to a stalwart built man in a coverall uniform. "Sorry," said Noah, "I didn't remember when you said you'd be here yesterday." Mason carried a toolkit at his side. "Please come in."

Mason's eyes took Noah in and he was taken aback by the flannel pajama bottoms. "I hope I didn't wake you."

Noah tightened his robe belt. "No, of course not, don't be silly."

Mason froze with a thousand-yard stare. He saw Donn sat atop the staircase. Chest hair poked out from Donn's bathrobe—even his boxer briefs were visible from the right angle. Noah entered Mason's gaze. "I'll show you the issue we've been having," said Noah. Mason nodded and took Noah's lead, but his eye lingered on Donn for a second too long.

Noah brought him to the sunroom. "Here it is," he said. "I already changed the bulb. Didn't seem to do the trick."

Mason dropped his things. "Seems simple enough."

Noah crossed his arms. He watched Mason move, slow and deliberate, like the man anticipated something. Perhaps he wanted to be left alone.

"Need me to show you where the breaker box is?" asked Noah.

"Like I said, I did some work for the previous owners."

"Right," said Noah. The toolbox snapped open. "Any idea why they sold the place?"

"Nope."

Noah clasped his palms together in an awkward clap. "Alright then," he said. "Let me know if you need anything." He stopped before getting out of earshot. "We might be out. To go to the store." Mason did not look back. He just rummaged through tools. "You have my number, right? In case you need us."

Mason gave a thumbs up.

"Great. I'll leave you to it."

Noah found Donn in the kitchen. He had already changed into pants and a button-up shirt. "He was strange," said Donn.

"Who was?"

"The handyman."

Noah grimaced. As if an insult to one Midwesterner was a snub on his character as well.

"People are strange everywhere. He's just quiet." He opened the fridge. All they had were ketchup packets and a water filter. "Do you want to drive to the store? Maybe buy some sweet corn?"

"Really?" asked Donn. He lowered his tone. "You want to leave him alone here?"

"This is a small town," said Noah. "The man has a reputation to uphold. I doubt he's here to cause any trouble." He grabbed Donn by the waist. "After all, the driver recommended him to me and Jim was nice." His eyes zeroed in, with a glint of gaiety, as Donn looked askance. He planted kisses along the nape of Donn's neck, then spoke softly in Donn's ear. "Besides, I don't want to sit around waiting for him on our first day."

"Yeah..." Donn's voice trailed in thought. "Or we could use dial-a-ride and I could meet your new townie friend."

Noah shot a questioning glare.

"What? I figure I should get to know this guy. If he really is the only driver in town he's bound to pick us up from a restaurant or bar at some point."

Noah figured Donn had a point. If they did not play nice with the locals this year, they would have an uphill battle for every year that proceeded. "Yeah," said Noah. "I don't see why not."

Noah and Donn climbed in the back of Jim's station wagon. The car reeked of residual hamburger grease and tobacco spit. Jim grinned and said, "Nice to see you again, Mr. Sanders." He reached a hand back for Donn to shake. "And good morning to you, sir. I don't believe we've met. I'm Jim." Donn shook. "You are?"

"The other Mr. Sanders, but you can call me Donn."

Jim's handshake went limp in Donn's grasp. "Oh." His knuckles clenched the steering wheel. "Oh, I see," he said. "I could've sworn you said you had a wife. That's all."

Donn turned to Noah, mouth agape. "Did you?"

Noah shook his head. "Of course not."

"No, no," said Jim. "I'm sure he's right." He prodded his temple with his index finger. "My memory isn't what it used to be."

Donn nodded, but his eyes drifted out the car window. Farmhouses and scud clouds flew by them, as Noah fingered the change in his pocket. He felt Donn's dubiety radiate in the backseat. He prayed the ride would end without another word spoken.

The storefront came into view. Donn leaned forward. The American heartland had some charm after all. There was nostalgia to the idea of a small business persisting in these times. "This is cute," said Donn. "So quaint."

Jim snickered. "We work with what we've got around these parts."

The car pulled into a parking spot and the couple thanked Jim for the lift. They entered the store, arm in arm, to find a cockle-skinned man behind the counter. His nametag read Mr. Carter.

"Good morning," Noah greeted.

Mr. Carter grunted in response. He waddled around the counter and stayed within six paces from them. "What brings you folks in today?"

"We're just looking," said Donn.

The aisles, which were stocked the day before, had been ransacked and left bare. Mr. Carter looked down his nose at them as they shopped. His plus lens glasses only magnified those watchful eyes. Noah elbowed Donn, then nodded in the shopkeeper's direction. Donn did not turn around. His head was locked in place. "We don't get many visitors," said Mr. Carter. "What brings you to town?"

Noah avoided eye contact. "We have a vacation home in town."

"You came too early then," said Mr. Carter. "We're still in tornado season."

"So I've been told." Noah kept walking with Donn and Mr. Carter in tow. "We were thinking about getting some of that sweet corn your wife told me about yesterday." Noah and Donn turned a corner. The rattan baskets were empty. "Oh. You're already out?"

Mr. Carter picked up a basket and dropped it. "Stuff like that gets picked off quick these days." He kicked the basket at Noah's feet. His guffaw reverberated off stark walls, then came to an abrupt end. "Good crop is hard to come by." He cracked a yellow smile. "Just like people, am I right?"

Noah and Donn exchanged a wide-eyed glance. "I suppose I missed my chance," said Noah. "We'll be going now. Thanks anyway." They headed to the front of the store. "We don't want to keep Jim waiting."

"Jim?" Mr. Carter leaned on a liquor shelf. "He left."

Donn checked the window. He ran outside. There wasn't a car in sight. Only open grassland and a cloud of dust rolling over the horizon. His hands balled into fists. "That little prick." He muttered.

Noah burst through the door. "What are we going to do?" he asked. "Jim stranded us in the middle of nowhere."

"Call him back," said Donn. Noah dialed the number from his app. "There must be some sort of misunderstanding here."

Noah scoffed. "So far the only misunderstanding here is your mother's estimation of these people." He wagged a finger in the shopkeeper's direction. "Did you see how that man treated us? Like we're shoplifters." His hands fell to his hip. "They're bumpkins." Thunder rumbled. Rain clouds rolled by in the distance. "I knew we should've done our own research before buying this place."

The line trilled in Noah's ear. "Sorry I can't make it to the phone right now," said Jim's voicemail. Noah felt an alert vibrate in his palm. His phone was low on battery power. He cursed under his breath. He threw his hands over his head and asked, "What now?"

Gray clouds funneled from above in a spiraled descent. Darkness enveloped the solar noon. Donn breathed in the still air. He knew the way home. "We don't have much of a choice." He stretched his legs. "Now we walk."

Noah and Donn stumbled up the driveway with their clothes caked in grime and an ache in their calves. The breeze picked up. Noah buttoned his cardigan. A windstorm was in the offing. Donn unlocked the door and stepped inside, but kept his eyes lowered to his feet dragging on the floor. All the natural light was drained by the blackened sky. Noah flipped a light switch, but nothing happened. He tried another switch and got the same result. Again and again until he realized there was no electricity in the house.

Noah became still. "You've got to be kidding me." His words came as a whimper. He called Mason's number from his call history. Noah stared at his phone screen. The call did not go through. He crossed his fingers and gave the call button another go.

The automated voicemail blasted from speakerphone. He tried again. This time someone picked up. Mason cleared his throat on his end of the line. "Hello," he said.

Noah sighed. "Hello, this is Noah Sanders. My husband and I just got home and it appears you left us without any power," he said.

"Yeah. Sorry about that. I had to get out of there before the storm." A car engine revved in the background. "I'll be back first thing in the morning."

"No," said Noah, "that is unacceptable. You need to return now. I won't stand for this. I have never—" His phone died.

"Let's just take it easy," said Donn. "I'm sure there's some sort of—"

"Let me guess," said Noah, "this is all another misunderstanding?"

"How else do you explain what's going on?" he asked.

"We're under attack."

"From who? No one knows us here."

Noah shook his head. "What is it going to take for you to realize what's happening, for you to stand up for us as a family?"

Donn marched at Noah like a soldier on a mission. As the final step in his stride, he stole a kiss from Noah—his husband's head cupped in his hands. Noah sank into his touch. "Listen," said Donn, "we are a family." Their lips, still dry and cracked, met once more. "I'd do anything for you. I love you."

"Leave with me then." Noah pulled away. His eyes darted from the front door to the garage. "We'll take the rental car and find the nearest motel for the night."

"Now?" Donn nodded outside, to the trees bent by high winds. The great oaks lurched towards the house in a bow. "We're in the middle of a severe weather warning."

"We have earthquakes and forest fires back home. We've been through worse than this. The storm is the least of our worries," said Noah. Thunder cracked and lightning illuminated the fear on his face. "I'm leaving. That much I've decided." He grabbed Donn by the hand. "Will you come with me?"

Donn closed his eyes and trembled. "Yes. Of course I will." He opened his eyes to find Noah's baby blues only inches away. "I could not bear to be without you."

Noah brought Donn out in the open and rushed into the driver's seat. He waved Donn in, but Donn noticed the Tahoe tilted to one side. Donn bent over to check. The front tire on the passenger side leaked out air in an audible hiss. "That's odd," he said. The back tire was flat too. A two-inch nail jutted out from the tread. "I'm sorry, babe." The color washed from Noah's face. "Looks like I hit a couple of nails on the drive in."

Noah threw his hands up in a fit. "This can't be happening."

Rainfall pelted the windows in thick beads, then pitter-pattered to a trickle and came to a standstill. "Right now," said Donn, "it's safest to hunker down." Noah's sullen eyes stared past Donn and to the house. He went back inside with his head hung. "We won't be going anywhere tonight."

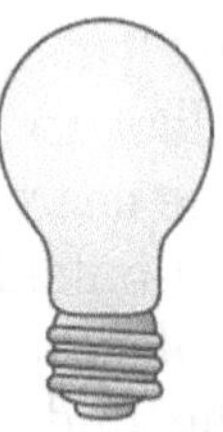

Crystal glassware on the living room table shimmered under the dim light of a dollar store candle. Donn uncorked a bottle of red wine and poured two glasses to the brim. He gave one to his husband. "A toast to our summer home?"

Noah swirled the wine before he took a swig. "This would pair well with blue stilton cheese," he said. "Too bad we didn't get any from the market."

Donn chuckled. "Don't tell me you're missing the locals now."

Noah shrugged. "At the moment, I'd miss anyone if it meant they'd give me a wheel of blue stilton." They laughed.

Donn gulped down saltine crackers with a swash of Port. "Remember when we got snowed in at a ski lodge in Utah?" He placed his hand near his husband's. Noah smiled. "That blizzard went on for forty-eight hours," said Donn.

Noah withdrew his hand from Donn's. "I remember," said Noah. "I also remember the beach, real shops, and a house where we didn't fear our neighbors. Our home."

Donn stood behind Noah to rub his shoulders with one hand and drink with the other. "Don't be resentful," said Donn. He worked Noah's stiff neck muscles. "We can only blame ourselves for being in this position." Wind seeped through the walls in wan howls. "They warned us this was coming."

"The locals?" Noah rolled his eyes. "Don't listen to a word they say."

"Why not? They were right."

"Yeah, conveniently so."

A mechanized moan cut off Donn's reply. Sirens blared across the plains from a mast posted a few miles off. Red ripples surfaced in their Port wine glasses. Donn kicked the chair out from under him and jumped to his feet. "What do we do?" he asked.

Noah blew out the candles and took his husband by the hand. "Get to the basement," he said. His head cocked from left to right—still unfamiliar with the layout. Thunderbolts guided his path in a pale blue light. Donn followed him downstairs, where they hid in the wine cellar. There, the siren's shriek came in muffled. The room was buried a foot below the frost line.

Noah and Donn huddled together in the corner. Their fingers intertwined, like laces in a knot, beside corked bottles of Madeira and Merlot. Noah was not present. His eyes were fixed on a champagne label, but he stared into the void. "We should have never allowed that ape into the house."

"Mason?"

"That yokel popped our tires," said Noah. "I bet if you check the breaker box he tampered with that too."

Donn flashed a quick smile and lifted his head to the ceiling. "I don't believe that," he said. "It's a tornado." Gales crashed against the siding like turbulent waves on a boat's hull. "We're all in this together."

"Believe it." Noah pinched his eyelids together in a crinkled fold. "They're full of hate and bigotry. They want people like us dead."

A strange sonance washed over them in a downpour of small vibrations—like droplets of a waterfall. Donn hushed his husband. "It's too late to concern ourselves with them now," he said. "We're all alone out here."

The front door splintered into slivers on the entryway floor. The chandelier fell, from a five-foot drop, onto the hardwood floor. Glass shards erupted from window frames in a glinted cascade. Noah hunched down and lowered his head to the floor. "They're coming," he cried. Donn tightened his hold on Noah's hand. Donn kissed his husband and said, "I love you." A stampede of noise tore through the house and tumbled down towards them in a dull roar. "No matter what comes next, stay with me."

ANATOMY OF THE UNIVERSE AND US

by Kiersten Adams

Ivory castanets hung from the cosmos like a mobile, and soft sounds coated in celestial sediment fell gently home. We watched from below as the universe bred old joints, sticking together to make tibias and fibulas. Pieces of the andromeda galaxy squeezed thighs and Pluto kissed soft bellies. Bodies start their annual plummet from grace back to earth like puzzle pieces, they recollected themselves from the fragments of their memories. Gingerly, noses and lips were placed along the route paved by their eyes. Sprouting like bamboo shoots, strands of hair cascaded down ribbed backs, twisting and curling themselves into locs of mocha and charcoal.

Watchers gazed up from the shoreline of the river, mesmerized by dancing bones. *She* sat among the others on the water and waited for the collection of her genealogy to take shape. Straddling the board of her catamaran, the pendulous engine swung with every ripple. The engine purred as the lunar panels were pleased by the sudden increase in activity. Isolated acts of re-creation were personified by knock-knees, double chins, and too large of ears. As they peddled down to moss-covered riverbanks, the former stars shed their outer layer and become a forest of Black and brown bodies, moist and ashy skin; overwhelming the boondocks as they assembled. The newly formed class passed smiles and secrets of Saturn and Jupiter amongst themselves. Finally rooted to the earth, they began their annual parade through the country, led by wistful women. Mothers held tight to the hands of young children, scooping wailing infants into their arms as the procession led them over moonlit waters.

Told as children to 'mind the song and dance of the dead,' many onlookers averted their eyes, shunning relatives as they cleared a path for the Black bone symphony. The river woke as families marched steadily over the water, sending fish sprinting with every step. Engines started up and boats flocked to shore, leaving *her* curious and alone. *She* twisted the handles to her catamaran and got into a low crouch, as *she* rode behind the parade. Along the shore, bodies broke away from the gaggle of the group and began to frolic through the wet fields of clay. Elderly men placed withered hands on dead trees, and watched as new buds sprouted from branch to branch. Moon-faced uncles with skin like burnt sugar hummed soft and low, offering the crows a new tune. Grandmothers bent with tired knees and lay kisses upon the soil, beneath their lips roses bloomed. *She* brought her catamaran to a slow pace as she neared feverish sounds of jubilee. Nestled in the branches of a dead poplar tree, she left her transport to charge as *she* took shelter out-of-sight behind a lean-to that smelled of hushpuppies and beignets.

The metro-hinterlands, once dormant through mid-summer slumber, came to life with the sounds of nostalgia once again. Despite the years of melancholy the War of 44' created in New Orleans, the returning residents smiled and praised the thick swaps and glass-stained beaches that encompass the boonies. Hidden, *She* listened to the harmonious bones as they *jangled* and *clicked* through the neighborhood. Homes that normally stood dimly lit had their lights extinguished, blinds pulled closed and ancestors meandered their homeland alone. Poking a head over a rickety fence into someone's yard, a stout little boy with a deep gash that ran from his widow's peak down to the corner of his lip attempts to pluck honeysuckle from a nearby bush.

"Come on now, you know you ain't s'posed to be doing'nat," an older woman scolds, pulling at the boy's arm and holding his hand as she led him down verdant roads. Not alone in his curiosity, others couldn't help but knock against homes that contained their remaining pedigree. They sifted through trash and wandered into empty barns. *She* followed behind, still cautious to remain hidden. Peeking from behind a lopsided stack of homes made from bright blue shipping crates, she eyed a shirtless man with molded splotches of gray and black near his heart. He kicked a long pole wrapped in solar panels.

"A Marley made this one, that's for sure," he said, summoning saliva from the back of his throat and hawking it into the dirt. From it quickly grew a patch of thick green grass. "That's some of my handy work, I can tell you that. Must'a been Juniper who taught Frankie 'bout his daddy's skills with a wrench. Yes ma'am, that there is some fine Marley doing," he regaled as he inspected the base of the structure.

"Leave it be Oz, before you break it." Another woman with a shaved head and baby at her breast called. The infant suckled and kicked in its mother's arm, plump little legs quivering with excitement. Others began aggressively studying the remnants of what they brought to the boondocks; solar-powered ships, compost bikes, and steam engine generators. Elders nodded in satisfaction at the progress of their own creations.

She shifted from one tired leg to the other, determined to see everything the cosmos brought back to earth. *She* hadn't realized in watching the bodies, one had taken an interest in her and came to stand at her backside. Tapping at her hip bone for long-overdue attention.

"Now you and I both know you ain't to be out here tonight," a rough voice whispered, reaching down and pulling *her* up by the shoulder. "You 'oughta be inside, I know your mother woulda told you that."

Spinning around, *She* squeezed *her* eyes shut, under *her* breath *she* muttered apologies in every tongue she had.

"Please, forgive me. *Perdóname. Lo siento. Perdóname,*" she whispered. There was a raspy laugh, followed by the feeling of a warm embrace. The type of warmth only a mother could produce. Letting her eyelids flutter open, *She* stared at broad forearms, sagging skin, and deep white tiger lines drawn on the inside of her forearms. *She* squinted at the elder as if catching a glimpse of the sun. An older woman with a sharp jaw and a head full of unkempt wild spirals held her gaze. Lines settled around her eyes and mouth, deep and rich, the elder woman didn't seem to notice the cosmogonic glow that enshrouded her.

"You gon speak or am I to rip the words out ya mouth?" the older woman asked, furrowing her brows.

"I wanted to see it," *She* stuttered out.

Wrapping her arm around the girl's shoulders, the elder star led *her* into the streets with the rest of the bone party.

"Well, here it is." Her elder gestured toward the parade. "This what you wanted to see? A bunch of dead folks tryna live," the elder said, standing unimpressed but amused by the sight of people skipping and running through streets covered in wild flora, picking and pruning through flower beds that sat untended outside folks' homes.

"I didn't think ya'll be so happy."

"What did you expect? A meteor shower with each rock holding a face of fury? For skeletons to tear the flesh from your bones out of jealousy? No baby, this our home too, we not coming to disrupt y'all's peace, just after our own," the elder replied, rubbing her arm gently as they marched on.

"My mama said that we had to send y'all away because from here, you'd have a harder time finding where you 'suposed to go. So why come back?" *She* asked, lifting her head to face the stars that still lingered above. The elder didn't say anything right away, just pulled *her* along with the rest of the ritualists. Walking towards the outskirts of the hamlet where green gobbled the land. The congregation swept through tall grass and thickets of thorn bushes. Men, women, and children; lovers and neighbors all shook hands and clapped backs, kissed cheeks, and squeezed one another before spreading themselves to the North, South, East, and West.

She and the elder watched as one man, cradled in the arms of his partner, laid together in the grass. The two men held hands and whispered prayers into each other's lips. The elderly woman and her companion stopped just short of them, pulling from the earth a sheet of soil. With shaking hands, the elder threw the sheet over the men's bones; the two lovers closed their eyes, and allowed themselves to be buried under the blankets of verdure. Like butter on hot concrete, Black skin faded into a luscious forest green before disappearing completely back into the earth.

"You do the next one," the elder called back, ushering *her* into the field where they covered the remaining bodies. *She* watched as babies buried their faces in the crook of their mother's necks before being covered. As one father, with a broad chest and several missing digits, took his son into his lap, and folded himself over, creating a small hill of green. A young girl, not much older than *her*, was buried laughing and doing the spread eagle. The rise and fall of her belly remained even once she had been rooted to the ground and covered. As they went about covering the once lost bones of their community, the elder woman sang out, in a deep baritone voice, the guiding song:

Where do you go when the earth is hot and the ground that keeps you has started to rot? The stars...

Where do you go when the waters rise, and mothers smother babies to stop their cries?

The stars...

Where do you go when there ain't no living, ain't no way that many of us will see another day?

The stars...

Not where gravity keeps us bound, where a joyless melody is the only sound.

The bells of war keep us awake,

And we pray to the Lord for our souls to take.

So listen children, learn to fly, abandon your woes for the endless Black sky

Hugged by the moon and kissed by Mars,

Find your rest amongst the stars.

As the last body is draped in green, the older woman catches her breath before taking a seat in a bed of sweetgrass, where she pulls an arm behind her head and rubs her bare feet into the earth.

"I missed this," The elder remembers, she stuck her big toe into the dirt and began to laugh. *She* stands next to her elder's relaxed body ready to blanket; but instead, comes to lay beside the larger woman, inching closer to her warmth. The elder pulled the young girl onto her breast and massaged circles into her scalp, lovingly and tender. In stillness, the older woman hummed the tune of her hymn behind her song, memories of a world that crumbled at her feet and drowned her in devastation flashed ahead. She remembered the world before, even when she tries to forget. Through her memories though she finds *her*. Small and curious, a near and distant relative, carrying on her ancestral teachings; someone to sing her song, and guide her home. There was a break in breath and silence.

"You never answered my question," *She* reminded the elder. "Ain't sleeping with the universe a little like Heaven?" *She* whispered. The elder laughed, leftover joy bubbled in her chest.

"You'd think so, huh. Maybe it did feel like that for a time. Floating through space, bumping against galaxies I ain't never heard of. It was beautiful."

"Then why come back?" *She* asked.

"It ain't home."

She thought of the swamps and foul smelling rivers. Then thought of the aimless drifting through a derelict void, of Pluto and other small wonders spit up by the cosmos.

"I still think it would've been better than here," *She* says, coming back to her delicate grooming.

"I've seen the universe in its entirety, little love, and none of it compares to you."

They laid together, two patches of an intergenerational quilt, silent and still. Nestled at the breast of *her* elder who summoned the stars. Who constructed from bone marrow a route back to earth. To her love land.

FERRYMAN

by E.D. Jones

I lay in the bunk, Gibson's arm around me as he snored in my ear. Outside the porthole, the blackness of space, spinning, empty, endless. Ahead of us, in under a week, Gibson's death by firing squad.

This went sideways...

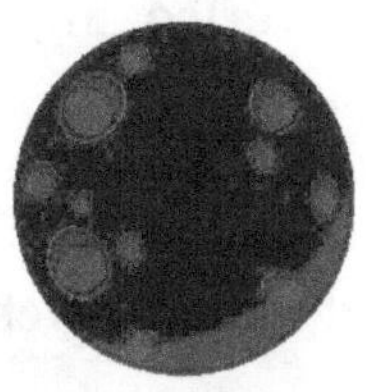

"The job is simple," General Haight said, sitting across from me in his office. "Escort the prisoner to Earth for execution. You know what he's done, and you know what he's capable of. Can you handle it?"

"Yes," I said. *For the right price.*

"I know you're a certified pilot," said the general, "but we need more than that."

He leaned back in his chair.

"Your last contract was with the Reds, right?"

"Yes, sir. I was hired to fight with their auxiliary regiment. All mercs. Just there if we were needed. We were."

"That was nasty," he said. "But your superiors said you acquitted yourself well – no sentimentality, no nonsense. You set the nationalists back decades, right?"

"Not my area," I said. "I just did what I was paid to do."

"Well, the same applies here," he said. "You're going to be locked in an airtight box with a notorious terrorist for three standard months, traveling from Mariner City back to the homeworld. You can't let him get inside your head."

"I know."

"And you can handle it."

"Yes," I said. "If the contract's good."

"25,000," he said.

I blinked. It'd be enough to buy a burrow of my own, maybe with a window overlooking Olympus Mons.

"I'm interested," I said.

"Well, then you've got the job," said the general. "Honestly, you're the most qualified applicant we've had. And you passed every psychological profile we threw at you."

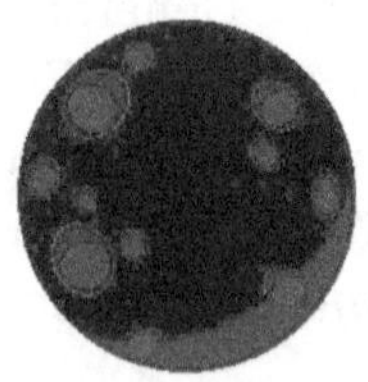

Two standard weeks later, I sat strapped into the cockpit, my prisoner restrained in a bunk behind me. He hadn't spoken since he'd been loaded aboard. I looked back at him. *Nathan Gibson. The man who'd bombed the terraforming research dome.* I didn't care why he'd done it. He'd been sentenced to death for treason against the homeworld, and that was that.

I closed my eyes and braced as the countdown ended. The rocket roared to life, pushing me back into my seat. Minutes later, we were in space, burning for the blue marble.

I unstrapped and started the spin drive, settling down to what was now the floor. As we got closer to Earth, I would increase the spin gradually, until we reached a full g a week before we hit the atmosphere. That'd help us acclimate to Earth gravity – critical for me, since I'd mostly grown up on the Red Planet.

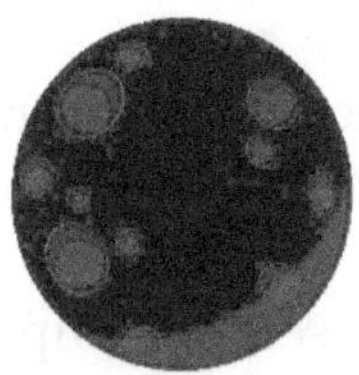

It was during his daily hour of exercise that the prisoner first spoke to me.

"You know why I did it, right?" he said, as I unstrapped him, helped him sit up, and cuffed his hands behind him. His voice was soft and sad, the embers of a fire that had once lit the imaginations of a thousand fanatics.

"I didn't mean to hurt anyone," he went on. "I just had to—"

"Send a message? You did. And here we are." I led him to the treadmill. He stepped on and started walking, his eyes downcast.

"The dome was supposed to be empty," he said after a few more minutes. "I had bad intel."

"And now a dozen scientists are dead," I said. "Suffocated by the raw atmosphere of Mars."

"I know," he said. "I'll never forgive myself for that."

"Neither will anyone else."

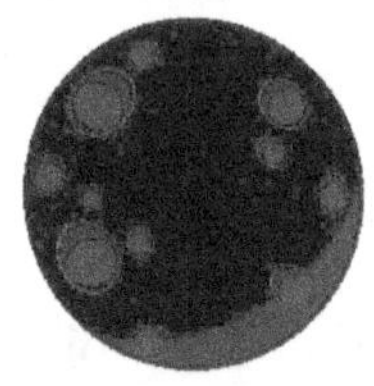

"I can't escape," he said. It was a week later, and he lay strapped into his bunk. I was studying a maintenance checklist.

"True," I said.

"Maybe I don't need to be strapped down all the time. Where am I going to go?"

"Nowhere," I said.

"So you want to loosen these up a bit?"

"No."

He sighed. "Come on, man..."

I looked over at him, meeting his eyes, seeing the defeat there, but also the desperation, and maybe a little fear. Here was a human being, on his way to the gallows. Yes, he'd killed a dozen scientists. And maybe that meant he deserved his punishment. I wasn't his judge, his jury, or his executioner. I was merely his ferryman.

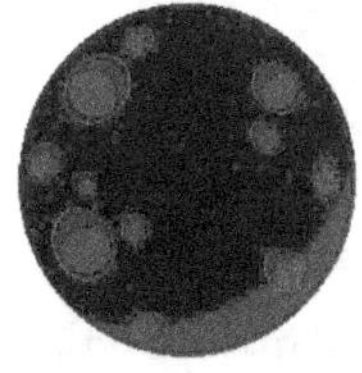

"Do you have any family of your own?" he asked me a few days later, as he walked on the treadmill.

"Just me," I said.

"Parents still alive?"

"No. Died in a...you know what? You don't get to know that." Anger rose in me. The gall of this terrorist, thinking he was entitled to know anything about me. Especially that memory. That memory was mine.

"Sorry," he said. "Just—"

"Just nothing," I spat. "Keep walking, stop talking."

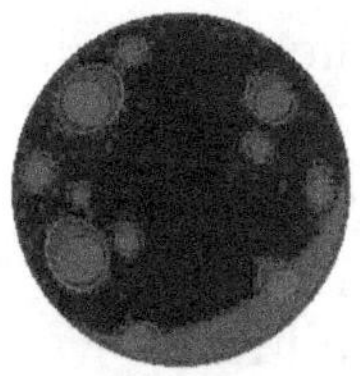

I monitored the instrument panel, triple checking that we were on course, no fuel leaks, no micrometeorite impacts.

Soft snoring behind me. I looked back, seeing the prisoner asleep on his back with his mouth open.

He's so young, I thought. Couldn't have been more than 30 standard years old, and probably younger than that.

In another timeline, I might have found Nathan Gibson attractive. Might have bought him a drink if I'd seen him in a bar.

In another timeline.

"What?" His voice startled me.

"What what?"

"You were staring at me."

"Making sure you're still breathing," I said. "Go back to sleep."

"Ok," he said. I heard a smirk in his voice. I ignored it.

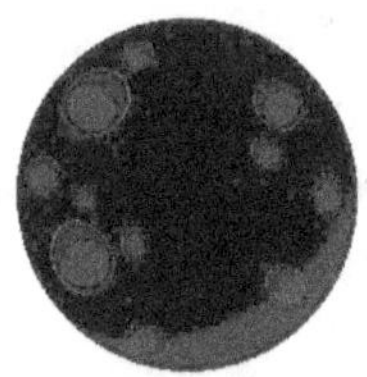

"You know who owned those terraformers I destroyed?"

I guided him to the treadmill. He stepped on and started walking.

"Mobsters," he said.

"What?"

"Mobsters. They infiltrated every part of the Martian government. The whole thing's corrupt."

"Where's your evidence?" I asked, and regretted it. I shouldn't get sucked into his propaganda.

"Destroyed," he said. "I have nothing. My whole network is gone. They were very efficient."

"Ah, the mythical 'they' that all conspiracy nuts love to point to," I said.

"It's not mythical. Think about it. How—"

"Even if you're right," I said, "How does blowing up a dome and killing a dozen scientists help your cause?"

"I keep telling you," he said, his voice a caged animal, "I didn't mean to kill anyone. Blowing up the dome was my only move. It was the only way to get people's attention."

"Yeah, well, you got people's attention, but not to the benefit of your cause," I said.

"I know. I failed. It was a bad plan. And I'll carry the pain and the guilt of it..."

He trailed off.

I was glad he felt guilty. That meant he had a little bit of humanity left in him.

Hadn't I done worse things in my life? And for nothing more than a paycheck? How many widows had I created during the conflict between the Reds and the Nationalists? Was it worse to kill if you don't even believe in the cause you're fighting for? Or does murder have the same moral value no matter the reason?

I'd struggled with this question before, but the paychecks had been good enough that I'd been able to bury it.

"You've been quiet for a few minutes," he said, stepping off the treadmill.

"True," I said.

"Thinking about anything in particular?"

"Yes."

I guided him back to his bunk.

"You sure you can't loosen these straps?" he asked. I looked back from the pilot's chair. I felt a little pity for him, wondered if it was actually sympathy.

I got up from the pilot's chair and knelt beside his bunk. Gibson's arms were irritated where the straps had rubbed against his skin. And honestly, what was the harm? What, was he going to knock me out, take control of the ship, and fly it...where? There wasn't enough fuel to get back to Mars, and Earth and Luna weren't exactly places one could land a ship undetected.

I raised an eyebrow at him.

"I promise to be on my best behavior," he said.

"I promise to kill you if you try anything," I responded.

"Understood," he said.

I unstrapped him from the bunk and stepped back. He sat up, rubbing his arms, and stretched.

"Thanks," he said.

I said nothing, returning to the captain's chair.

"Do you have any books or anything?" he asked.

I had brought a library of new Martian fiction. I grabbed the notebook off the shelf and handed it to him.

"Ah, the new Gertrude Booth novel," he said. "Been waiting for this one. You read it?"

"Not yet."

"She's such a brilliant worldsmith," he said.

"Did you say wordsmith?"

"Worldsmith. Creator of worlds," he said.

"Never heard that term."

"I might have just made it up."

"Well, it's not bad," I said.

We had two standard months to go.

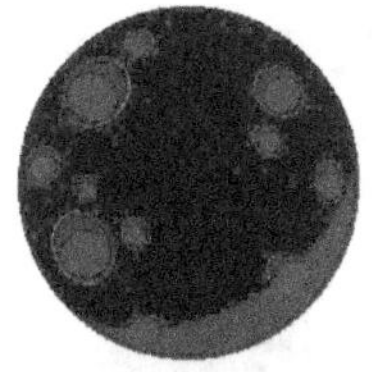

"They killed my husband," he said. I'd been daydreaming, staring at the blackness outside.

"What?"

"The cartel. They murdered him. I was getting too close. They'd threatened before, but Brad kept telling me he could take care of himself." His voice cracked like cheap glass. "I found him crumpled in an airlock with its door wide open to Mars."

"I'm so sorry," I said, and I meant it.

"That's why I had to escalate," he said, steel in his voice now. "Why I had to blow up the dome. I had to..." He broke off. I heard him suppress a sob.

Damn...

I wondered what I would do. But of course, I had no idea, and there was no way to speculate. Not really.

I felt myself drawn to him in that moment, a vulnerable, scared human being, doused in tragedy and drowning in rage. I stood up from the captain's chair and sat next to him on the bunk.

What am I doing?

I saw him again, the monster who'd murdered twelve innocent scientists.

What am I doing?

I studied him. A tear fell and spun in the Coriolis forces before gravity pulled it down.

That night, as I lay in my bunk, I thought about a lot of things. About how people are driven to extremes.

About how someone can end a life without even knowing it.

Or just for a paycheck.

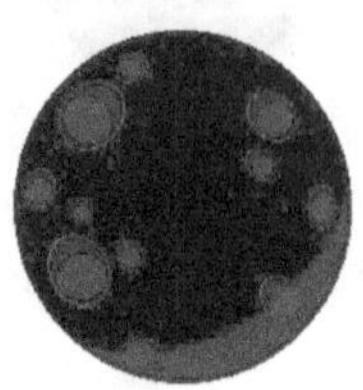

It was a few days later when he first tried to kiss me. I realized how much I'd let my guard down with him. We were sitting on his bunk. A month separated us from his execution.

"We flew to Mars because we wanted that frontier spirit back," he said. "We knew that if we worked together, we could tame the wilderness there just like we did on the homeworld. But people take their garbage with them, and...look at me, I'm making a speech at you," he said.

"No, it's ok," I said.

"I came to Mars as a kid, on one of the first caravans after Mariner City was declared airtight and fit for life. I was among the first humans to take off a helmet in the city. That mattered to me. But as I grew up, it became clear that the dream was corrupt, and there was a poison at the heart of it. That's what got...that's what made me..."

He trailed off. After a second, I said, "At least you believed in something. I just..."

"Killed for a paycheck? Let's not compare our sins," he said.

"But isn't that the point?" I asked. "I kill for a contract, and that's legal, and I get paid. You kill for a belief, and that's treason, and you get executed."

"We killed," he said. "It means the same thing either way."

He looked at me then, and a switch flipped in my mind. All thought of this man as a murdering terrorist washed out of me. He leaned toward me.

"I—" I stopped him. "Sorry. I'm..."

"It's ok," he said.

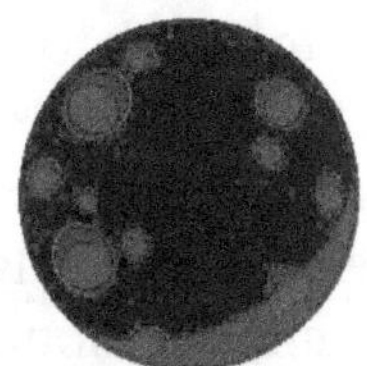

We filled the awkwardness with idle talk. He told me about his favorite music. I told him what I knew about Earth, and we ignored the black hole at the end of that thought.

But feelings always catch up.

It was a few days later. He'd just gotten off the treadmill, and I was leading him toward his bunk. I'd turned the spin up another notch, and we were both feeling the extra gravity. He lost his balance as he bent down to his bunk. He grabbed my shoulder, and I helped him sit. He leaned in and kissed me, and this time, I let him.

"I know," he said, breaking the kiss. "That was way out of line. But can't a dying man dream?"

"It's fine," I said, sitting beside him. Heat rose in me, two months of being cooped up in a box finally overriding any sense of propriety. I dove into him, and he rose to meet me.

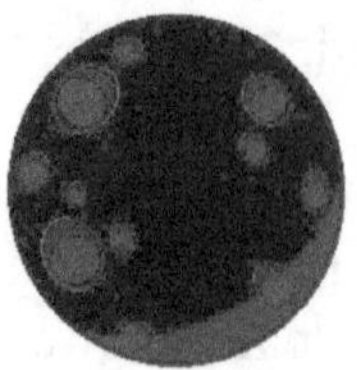

I thought about our journey, a week out from Earth, 1g of spin gravity pressing on me like a boot. I thought about what he'd come to mean to me, and the choice I had to make.

And I resented him for putting me in this position, where I had to make a moral judgment with a fierce headwind of unexamined emotions and newfound feeling. It wasn't a choice for me – it was a choice for him. Did I accept the coin and ferry him to his death? Did I refuse the coin and...what, run? Where would we run to? Why should I throw my life into chaos for this man I barely knew, who'd found someone to connect with at the most terrifying and vulnerable moment of his life?

"I know what you're thinking," he mumbled into my shoulder. He rolled over and lay on his back, his eyes open and clear.

"You have to turn me in," he said. "I can't ruin your life over what I did."

"And I don't know if I can hand you over," I said.

"You can," he said.

"But what if—"

"What if nothing. There's no escape that doesn't involve you and me running...for the rest of our lives.

You try to spring me, then your head's on the block just like mine is."

I had no response to this, because of course he was right.

"You asked about my family," I said.

"Yeah?"

"My parents..."

Pulling on that memory hurt. It hurt a lot.

"Something happened in our apartment, and it lost air. I was at work when I got the alarm. I came home and found the door sealed, and when I'd managed to repressurize the apartment, I found them." Images of my parents' grey, empty faces, lying in their bed, flashed in my memory.

Gibson was silent for a beat, and then said, "I'm so sorry."

"You said you were proud to be one of the first people to take a helmet off in Mariner City," I said.

"Yeah."

"Sometimes I wonder if that was such a good idea."

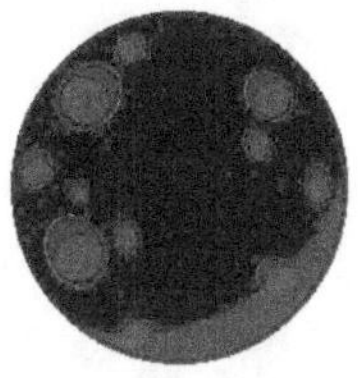

I set the craft for atmospheric entry. Ahead of me, the blue marble spun, majestic and glowing with the life I hoped Mars would see one day. Nathan Gibson lay strapped into the bunk behind me. I looked back at him. He smiled and gave me a thumbs up.

"Thanks," he said.

"For what?"

"For listening. For understanding. For giving a condemned man some companionship and comfort on his way out."

I nodded softly at him.

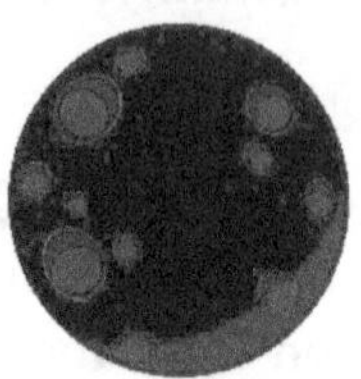

I watched as they wheeled him off the ship and took him to his cell, feeling a curious numbness.

After he'd gone, I stepped out of the capsule and breathed free air for the first time in my life. It smelled peppery, and it had a cold that bit at me.

An endless blue sky soared above me, streaked with clouds.

"Your payment is deposited into your account," said a man in a suit. "Thank you for your service."

"You're welcome," I said.

But not to him.

GOOD BYE

by Erin Edwards

I'd watched Kitty do this time after time, but I'd never properly taken note of how she arranged everything and where each candle went. The specific layout was probably important, but all I had to work from was my hazy memory and a few of Kitty's Instagram posts. I peered at the screen of my phone, trying to judge whether I'd accurately set the scene. Frowning, I made a few adjustments. One votive several inches to the left. The board straightened so it was dead centre.

Cleocatra blinked at me from across the board, judging me even as I reached out to scratch her under the chin. I'd been the one to name her, but Kitty had picked her out at the adoption shelter. Every witch needed a black cat, she'd insisted. I'd rolled my eyes but given in, as I always had. Cleo was the only thing that stopped the flat from going completely silent these days, her little bell tinkling in a constant reminder I wasn't alone. Whether or not she was a true witch's cat had been a matter of debate, but she'd always sat close while Kitty did her rituals, and now she was doing the same for me.

I picked up Kitty's lighter, the one I'd always teased her about for being decidedly un-witchy. The Bic had once been plain white, but she'd covered the whole thing in neon pink nail varnish and decorated it with stars in black Sharpie, going to the effort of refilling it every time it ran out. The designs were smudged from where her fingers used to grip it, and I held it tight for a moment before flicking it on. It was the closest I'd ever get to holding her hand again.

It wasn't clear whether there was an order I had to light the candles in for this to work. Praying this wouldn't be what ruined my attempt, I started with the one straight in front of me and worked my way around, slowly surrounding myself with glowing flames.

My hands shook as I lit the last wick, the flame seizing the opportunity to lick at my fingertips. I winced, but ignored the sharp burn as I set the lighter down, performing nonchalance for an absent audience. Cleo watched from a distance, flicking her tail. She knew to stay away from lit candles. Maybe she was a witch's cat.

The layout seemed right when I compared it one final time to Kitty's photograph, but there was something off about the whole thing. The room was too bright. I doubted ghosts minded whether lights were on or off, but I'd promised myself I'd take this seriously so, for the sake of dedication, I carefully stepped my way out of the circle of candles and flicked off the light switch.

It suddenly got a lot more real.

This was exactly the kind of thing I preferred to avoid - the candles, the Ouija board, the incense. This was Kitty's domain and I felt so out of my depth that the shaking in my hands got worse, creeping up my arms. But this was the only chance I had and I needed to at least try.

When I settled myself down in front of the board again, I knew I needed one last thing. It was easier to reach someone if you had something of significance. Kitty had explained it all to me a few months after my brother had died. She'd only asked me once if I wanted her to try to contact him for me. When I'd said no, she never mentioned it again. I felt almost guilty that I was trying for her when I hadn't tried for Danny, but I'd never felt this desperate to see someone again in my life. Kitty was my whole world.

I slipped the chain around my neck over my head, pooling it up just below the board so the ring threaded onto it nested on top of the pile. It had once been Kitty's, a gift from me last Christmas. Not an engagement ring, but a promise nonetheless. She hadn't taken it off once, until someone else had done it for her, putting it in a plastic bag with the rest of her personal effects.

With the ring in place, I couldn't put it off any longer. Either I was doing this, or I had to pack everything away and accept the fact Kitty was gone and I'd never see her or speak to her ever again. The second choice didn't feel like an option. Taking a deep breath and letting it out slowly, I prepared myself to look like an utter fool. At least I only had Cleo as a witness. I rested both my index fingers on the planchette.

"I call to the spirit of Katherine McKenzie," I said, my voice just about holding strong.

Nothing happened. The candles didn't flicker. Cleo didn't even blink.

I hadn't anticipated how disappointed I'd feel. Despite how I'd always proclaimed I didn't believe in any of it, I'd never had a reason to hope so fervently to be wrong before.

"Katherine McKenzie," I repeated, a quiver in my throat at her name. "I invite you in."

I could feel my heart beating in my throat as I waited for a response, my ears pricked for the tiniest noise. When not even a floorboard creaked, the corners of my eyes bloomed with hot tears.

"Please," I begged, losing the formal composure I'd always seen Kitty adopt for these things. "It's Sarah. I need you to tell me *I told you so*. I need you to prove me wrong, love. I need you. Please, Kitty."

As soon as her nickname crossed my lips, I felt a breeze against the back of my neck. Rather than the icy cold chill spirits always seemed to bring with them in horror films, it was a reassuring warmth, one I'd felt before – every time Kitty stepped up behind me to kiss my neck. The sensation was accompanied with the familiar sweet vanilla smell of her favourite body lotion. Every muscle in my body seized up as a gasp escaped my lips.

"Kitty?" I said, barely louder than breathing.

It had to be a coincidence. Or wishful thinking. Maybe I was just conjuring it all up in my head. I would have sold my soul for a single moment more with her, so I knew I was capable of tricking myself into feeling her presence. Only then, Cleo meowed, weaving her way through the candles to stretch out beside the board, rolling over onto her back with her paws up in the air. Like she always did when she wanted Kitty, and only Kitty, to rub her belly.

"Kitty, please tell me that's you?" I asked, half afraid there would be no answer.

Whenever Kitty had told me the planchette for the Ouija board just moved beneath her hands, I'd always rolled my eyes, kissed her cheek, and told her she was lucky she was cute. I owed her the biggest apology when I felt the wooden token shift under my fingers. I knew I wasn't guiding it, just nudging it along to give it enough force to get where it wanted to go, because it landed directly above the word **YES**.

I let out an unrestrained sob, my heart beating faster and faster as the tears collecting in my eyes grew heavy enough to fall. It took all of my effort not to take my hands off the board.

"Hello, my love," I managed through gasps. "I miss you."

The planchette shifted under my fingers again and I patiently waited as it spelled out the word **LOVE**. The sentiment was clear, even if the message was short. A breeze ruffled my hair, making the candles dance.

"Where are you?" I asked. "Are you in heaven?"

The planchette drifted across the board to **NO**. I paused for a moment, unsure.

"Are you in... hell?"

The candles flickered like it was her laughter fuelling them, the unmistakable hitch in the back of her throat in the lick of the flames. The planchette circled the **NO** inscription again and I let out a sigh of relief. I hadn't even realised I'd been worried about the possibility.

"I want you back," I admitted, tears now streaming down my cheeks. "You should still be here. We were supposed to get married and adopt so many more cats and you were going to do amazing things and show the world how wonderful you are, and now you can't, and I can't do it alone. I need you. I love you. It's not fair," I gasped, my lungs heaving as I stammered through each word. "It's just not fair."

When the planchette moved again, the letters it landed on spelled out **I KNOW**, then a pause, then **SORRY**.

I managed to force a laugh.

"It's not your fault," I assured her. She wasn't the one who'd been driving under the influence. The only person to blame was the man behind the wheel of the car that hit her, and he was just as dead and gone.

In spite of how much I'd been desperate for this to work, I hadn't really been expecting it to. I didn't have a list of questions to ask, even though there was plenty I wanted to know. Had Kitty ever planned on marrying me? Did she feel any pain before she died? What did she want me to do with her belongings? There were things I wanted to keep, if she'd let me, but I wasn't sure if there was anything she wanted to go to her parents or her sister. She hadn't made a will. No twenty-four year old should ever need one.

It was clear Kitty couldn't say much. Each movement of the planchette got weaker and weaker, needing more input from me to guide it across the board. It was only a matter of time before I wouldn't be able to discern her intentions anymore and all the movement would be my own.

"You need to go, don't you," I asked, the tears still falling. I hadn't stopped crying once.

When the planchette shifted across to **YES**, a sob heaved through my chest.

"Please stay," I tried. "I need you. Cleo needs you. It's too quiet, Kitty. Please."

A cocoon of warmth settled around me, like a hug I couldn't quite lean into. Cleo jumped up into my lap, wanting to be part of it. I had to reach around the bundle of fur to keep my fingers on the planchette as it moved across the board once again.

TOLD YOU SO

The noise I made was a cross between a sob and a laugh. It usually would have scared Cleo away, on the rare occasion I could coax her into being a lap cat, but she didn't even flinch. Her attention was fixed on something on the other side of the board. Cats were more sensitive to seeing spirits, Kitty had always told me. I would have given anything to have that kind of vision at that moment. Sensing Kitty was nothing short of a miracle, but being able to see her again, to touch her, was what I longed for most.

"You did tell me," I agreed. "I'm sorry I ever doubted you."

I felt the now familiar tug of the planchette moving and let Kitty guide me.

KEEP THE RING

There was a pause, and then the planchette shifted down right to the bottom of the board.

GOOD BYE

"No!" I protested. "Please, not yet."

The breeze brushed against my cheek, the candles flaring up brighter than they'd been all night.

"I'm not ready for you to go, Kitty! Please!"

I shouted the words through my tears. Kitty had never said anything about only being able to contact spirits once, but I got the sense this goodbye was final. It wasn't like I could check in with her every evening.

"I love you," I called out. "I will always love you."

I felt the warm breeze at the back of my neck one final time, the candles burning even brighter, just for a moment, before the flames collapsed into thin plumes of smoke, sending the room into darkness. My whole body was shaking, every limb feeling cold in the absence of Kitty's warm energy. It took me a few moments until I could find the strength to lift my fingers from the Ouija board, burying them in Cleo's fur in an attempt to stave off the icy chill.

With the candles extinguished, the only light came from the moon outside the windows. It fell across the board in a beam, glinting off Kitty's ring. I reached for the chain, pulling it back over my head and tucking it under my shirt so it could sit over my heart.

Surveying the scene in front of me, I wondered if it had really happened. I wanted it enough that I didn't doubt I could make myself believe, but it felt so real. I knew no one would ever believe me if I tried to explain. Not that I had any plans to share my last moment with Kitty with anyone. I scrubbed tears from my cheeks with the back of my hand, shifting Cleo off my lap so I could climb to my feet.

Collecting up one of the still-smouldering candles, I set it down on the windowsill where Kitty had always liked to read. The last book she'd started was still there, forever unfinished. I lit the candle again before placing the lighter down atop the book. I promised myself I'd always keep it burning, pressing my fingers to my lips. When I took a step back, Cleo winding herself around my feet, I watched as the flame flickered once, twice, then went still.

"Goodbye," I whispered, fresh tears replacing the ones I'd brushed away.

I picked Cleo up and held her close, surprised when I didn't even get an indignant meow for my troubles. It was just the two of us now. We'd have to learn to get by.

About the Authors

Lina Gerhard

Lina Gerhard is a scientific writer and neuroscientist by day and a fantasy writer by night. She lives in eastern Pennsylvania with her husband and furbabies, and when she's not busy sciencing and dreaming up fictional worlds, she's creating music and art, reading, or gaming. She loves to write about family relationships, atmospheric settings, and magic to make people dream, but most of all, she writes to help people feel less alone.

Marianne Xenos

Marianne Xenos is writer and visual artist living in western Massachusetts. She works with photography, collage and stories. Along with narratives about shapeshifters and urban dragons, Marianne is working on a fantasy novel set in Boston's queer community in 1983. She is a winner of the 2022 Writers of the Future contest. www.mariannexenos.com

Tucker Struyk

Tucker Struyk (he/him/his) is a queer writer and podcaster for *Hookswitch Hotline*. He has recently published pieces in *Orion's Beau, Not A Pipe Publishing*, and *13th Floor Magazine*. His piece "Our Father's Judgment" was published in the spring 2021 issue of *13th Floor Magazine*, where it was awarded an Editor's Choice Award, and his piece "Getaway" was given an honorable mention in the Fall/Winter 2022-23 issue of *Allegory*.

Katie Kent

Katie Kent is a writer of fiction and non-fiction living in the UK with her wife, cat and dog. She likes to write stories, mostly for a YA audience, particularly about LGTBQ characters, mental illness, time travel and the future—sometimes all in the same story! Her stories have been published in ***Youth Imagination, Limeoncello, Breath and Shadow*** and ***Northern Gravy***, amongst others, and in a handful of anthologies including ***The Trouble with Time Travel, Summer of Speculation: Catastrophe, Growth*** and ***My Heart to Yours***. Her non-fiction, mostly mental health-related, can be found in publications including ***The Mighty, You & Me Magazine, Ailment, OC87 Recovery Diaries*** and ***Feels Zine***. You can follow her on Twitter @uniKH80 and visit her website at
www.katiekentwriter.com

Gwen Tolios

Gwen Tolios is a queer author who settled in Chicago after time abroad. Writing short stories and novels, both fantasy and contemporary, she's known for building rich worlds and characters. When not chugging coffee or typing words, Gwen is on a multi-year quest to encourage her cat to cuddle with her. Progress is slow.

J.L. Henker

J.L. is a writer, blogger and avid reader of fantasy/sci-fi. She is currently doing final edits on a high fantasy novel, querying fantasy/sci-fi short stories and facilitating a support group for women fantasy writers. Her career has included book seller, used/rare book buyer and bookstore manager. She lives in northern California with her partner Diane and a very spoiled cat named Leo. Find out more at www.jlhenker.com.

E.D. Jones

E.D. Jones lives in Tulsa, Oklahoma with his husband and too many dogs. He writes sci-fi, horror, and weird fiction inspired by all the mad dreamers who create worlds out of words. His short story "Resolution" was published in an anthology called *On Loss*, and his story "Ferryman" first appeared as an audio production on the podcast *The Overcast*. E.D. writes a sporadically updated blog at www.sinisterblog.com and can also be found at Facebook.com/writesinister

Summer Jewel Keown

Summer is a recent transplant from Indianapolis to Ithaca, New York, both wonderful places with weather that can't decide what it wants to be from day to day. She writes mainly fiction – short stories, novels, and the occasional short play. Her day job is event planning, which allows her to indulge the Type-A side of her personality. In between, she lets roosters sit on her head, explores her new town, makes quilts, and has deep philosophical discussions with her dog and cat.

Kiersten Adams

Kiersten Adams is a freelance journalist interested in pop-culture, television, music, film, and anything absurd. A West Chester University 2020 graduate, Kiersten enjoys reading, writing, photography, trying to propagate her friends' plants, and getting into heated discussions on prison reform. As a Philadelphia native, she lets the city inspire her passion for writing.

Erin Edwards

Erin Edwards is a dedicated Londoner and compulsive writer. By day she works in archives, by night in a theatre auditorium, and in every spare moment in between she carves out time to write. With an inability to stick to a single genre or age group, the one constant in her work is that it is all unapologetically queer.
Erin's work had been featured in a number of lit mags and anthologies. She is currently balancing working on both a young adult historical romance and an adult speculative fiction novel. She can be found on Twitter (as long as it hasn't crashed and burned) at @EEdwardsWrites

ABOUT THE EDITORS

Fable Tethras

Fable Tethras is a journalist-turned-author who writes depressing science fiction and less depressing fantasy. Their short story, Shrinking, was awarded an honorable mention in the L Ron Hubbard's Writers of the Future Contest and is published in Not A Pipe Publishing's Anthology *Shout: An Anthology of Resistance Short Fiction and Poetry*. They live in Albuquerque, NM, where they spend most of their time writing or playing board games. Fable can be found on Facebook.

Viveca Shearin

Viveca started off as a freelance editor who joined Not a Pipe Publishing to work on a single novel and has worked her way to the top. In 2020 she was promoted to co-publisher and co-owner. She lives in Brooklyn, New York. When she's not working, Viveca can often be found with a big mug of tea (or coffee), her face buried in a good book or video game, and her beloved cat nearby for company.

Claudine Griggs

Claudine's fiction has appeared in Lightspeed, Escape Pod, Zahir Tales, New Theory, Leading Edge SF, Not a Pipe Publishing, Upper Rubber Boot Books, Mount Island, Ligeia, Flora Fiction, etc. Her story "Helping Hand" appears as an episode in the Netflix series "Love, Death & Robots." Her first novel, *Don't Ask, Don't Tell*, was released on June 1, 2020, and a book-length story collection, Firestorm, was released on March 13, 2022. She has two nonfiction books out regarding trans/gender issues as well.

Claudine is a long-time member of the Authors Guild and a member of Science Fiction Writers of America.